Planet Earth

Finding Balance on the Blue Marble with Environmental Science Activities for Kids

Kathleen M. Reilly

Illustrated by Tom Casteel

Titles in the **Environmental Science** book set

 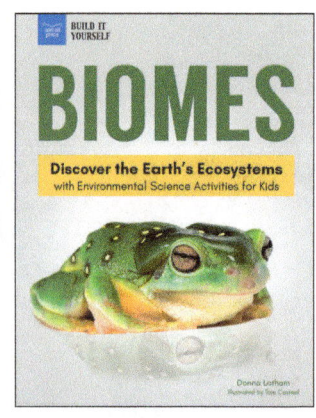 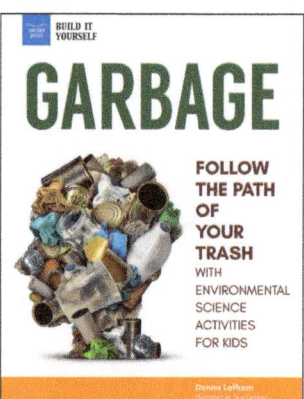 

Check out more titles at www.nomadpress.net

Nomad Press
A division of Nomad Communications
10 9 8 7 6 5 4 3
Copyright © 2019 by Nomad Press. All rights reserved.
No part of this book may be reproduced in any form without permission in writing from
the publisher, except by a reviewer who may quote brief passages in a review or **for limited educational use**.
The trademark "Nomad Press" and the Nomad Press logo are trademarks of Nomad Communications, Inc.

ISBN Softcover: 978-1-61930-743-8
ISBN Hardcover: 978-1-61930-740-7

Educational Consultant, Marla Conn

Questions regarding the ordering of this book should be addressed to
Nomad Press
2456 Christian St.
White River Junction, VT 05001
www.nomadpress.net

Contents

Timeline . . . iv

Introduction
Welcome to Planet Earth . . . 1

Chapter 1
Earth: Our Spot in Space . . . 6

Chapter 2
The Planet of Air and Water . . . 19

Chapter 3
Our Star, the Sun . . . 36

Chapter 4
Life on Earth . . . 47

Chapter 5
Pollution . . . 56

Chapter 6
Climate Change . . . 71

Chapter 7
Recycling . . . 87

Chapter 8
Finding the Balance . . . 99

**Glossary | Metric Conversions
Resources | Essential Questions | Index**

Interested in Primary Sources?

Look for this icon. Use a smartphone or tablet app to scan the QR code and explore more! Photos are also primary sources because a photograph takes a picture at the moment something happens.

 You can find a list of URLs on the Resources page. If the QR code doesn't work, try searching the internet with the Keyword Prompts to find other helpful sources.

planet earth

TIMELINE

2000 BCE: The Chinese first use coal as an energy source.

1543 CE: Nicolaus Copernicus explains that the sun is at the center of our solar system and the earth orbits the sun.

1609: Johannes Kepler describes the motion of planets.

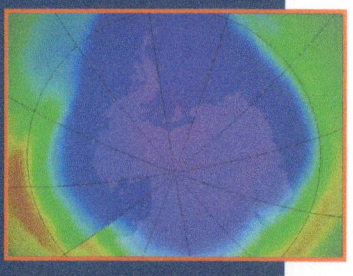

1750: Carbon dioxide (CO_2) in our atmosphere is 279 ppm (parts per million).

1820: The term *greenhouse effect* is first used by Joseph Fourier.

1882: The first hydroelectric dam is built by Thomas Edison near Niagara Falls in New York.

1890: The mass production of automobiles begins, creating a larger demand for gasoline.

1970: The first Earth Day is held in the United States on April 22.

1970: The Environmental Protection Agency (EPA) is created to implement federal laws that protect the environment.

1979: The first solar panels are installed on the White House.

1998: Carbon dioxide measurements in the atmosphere pass 350 ppm for the first time in human history.

TIMELINE

2010: The largest oil spill in the United States, from *Deepwater Horizon*, occurs in the Gulf of Mexico.

2011: The world's population reaches 7 billion people.

2013: *Solar Impulse*, the first airplane powered by solar energy, flies across the United States.

2016: The Paris Agreement is signed by 195 countries that pledge to reduce greenhouse gas emissions.

2016: The earth experiences its hottest year on record.

2017: The carbon dioxide level in the atmosphere stands at 405 ppm, the highest level in at least 800,000 years.

2017: U.S. President Donald Trump announces his intention to withdraw from the Paris Agreement.

How long will it take to biodegrade?

- **paper towel:** about three weeks
- **apple:** about two months
- **plastic bag:** about 20 years
- **tin can:** about 50 years
- **disposable diaper:** more than 400 years
- **glass bottle:** about 1 million years!

Introduction

WELCOME TO
PLANET EARTH

What's the world like outside your window? A grassy backyard full of trees? Maybe you have swaying palm trees or bending birches brushing gently against your window at night. Or maybe there aren't any trees, but dry, desert air drifts in through your screen door. Maybe pigeons gather on your window ledge, far above the urban streets below.

ESSENTIAL QUESTION

What type of environment do you live in? Desert, **tundra**, forest, grassland?

Whatever you see out your window—that's the **environment**. Everything natural that's out there, living and nonliving, is what people are talking about when they say "the environment." The grass, trees, birds, bugs, bears, falling rain, shining sun— even you! You're part of the environment, too.

PLANET EARTH

WORDS TO KNOW

urban: relating to a city or large town.

environment: everything in nature—living or nonliving—including plants, animals, rocks, and water.

tundra: a treeless Arctic region that is permanently frozen below the top layer of soil.

industry: the large-scale production of goods, especially in factories.

climate change: a change in long-term weather patterns, which happens through both natural and man-made processes.

The environment is the things you can see, such as animals, rocks, and water, plus all of the things you can't see, including earthworms pushing through the ground under your feet and the air that's touching your skin right now.

ENVIRONMENTAL PROBLEMS

Wherever you are on Planet Earth, you'll find the environment. And a thing as enormous as a planet must stay pretty healthy, right? After all, what could have enough strength to hurt an entire planet?

A beautiful mountainous environment here on Earth

In fact, many people are very worried about the health of the planet. For decades, scientists have been studying the impact people and **industry** have on the environment and how our habits, behaviors, and inventions affect the natural world.

It turns out that the planet is warming up. More than 97 percent of scientists around the world have found that **climate change** is real and at least partly caused by humans.

Take a look at an animated infographic that shows the progression of global temperatures for the last 116 years.

temperature circle climate

That means there's a direct link between human activity and rising temperatures.

Not everyone agrees with the scientists who are finding evidence of climate change. Some people believe that the warming is part of a natural cycle that humans have very little control over. Others don't believe that climate change is a very big problem. Others are suspicious of things they don't experience themselves. They think that if they live in a region that gets lots of snow, why should they believe that the overall temperature of the globe is rising?

PLANET EARTH

> **WORDS TO KNOW**
>
> **atmosphere:** the mixture of gases that surround a planet.
>
> **climate:** the average weather patterns in an area during a long period of time.
>
> **solar system:** the eight planets and their moons that orbit the sun.
>
> **global warming:** an increase in the average temperature of the earth's atmosphere, enough to cause climate change.

However, if we focus on scientific studies that have tracked global conditions for many decades, we see that the planet is breaking temperature records nearly every year. Our **atmosphere** is getting warmer, causing **climates** around the world to change. Extreme weather events, such as massive floods, wildfires, and mudslides, can be caused by climate change.

All of this points to the need to focus on ways humans can help the earth recover and thrive.

In *Planet Earth*, we'll take a look at everything that makes up the environment, from earth to air to water to animals. We'll get our hands dirty, feel the wind on our faces, and meet different creatures that live on land and in the ocean. We'll also consider the planet's place in the **solar system** among the sun, moon, other planets, all the asteroids, comets, and stars. Earth science is part of space science.

A mudslide in Southern California
credit: Air National Guard photo by Air Force Staff Sgt. Cristian Meyers

After we have a good idea about what the global environment is, we'll explore the issue of climate change and take a look at how **global warming** is affecting life on Earth. We'll also explore things we can do to help the planet stay healthy!

Let's get started!

Good Science Practices

Every good scientist keeps a science journal! Scientists use the scientific method to keep their experiments organized. Choose a notebook to use as your science journal. As you read through this book and do the activities, keep track of your observations and record each step in a scientific method worksheet, like the one shown here.

Question: What are we trying to find out? What problem are we trying to solve?	
Research: What is already known about the problem?	
Hypothesis/Prediction: What do we think the answer will be?	
Equipment: What supplies are we using?	
Method: What procedure are we following?	
Results: What happened? Why?	

Each chapter of this book begins with an essential question to help guide your exploration of Planet Earth and the environment. Keep the question in your mind as you read the chapter. At the end of each chapter, use your science journal to record your thoughts and answers.

ESSENTIAL QUESTION

What type of environment do you live in? Desert, tundra, forest, grassland?

Chapter 1

EARTH:
OUR SPOT IN SPACE

Imagine you're traveling across the **Milky Way**, closing in on a bright star. As you get closer, you realize it's our sun. Then, you pass some planets with familiar names—Saturn, Jupiter, Mars . . . all these are unique and interesting, but they're lacking something extra special: life.

And then you see Earth.

> **ESSENTIAL QUESTION**
>
> What are some of the ways the environment where you live maintains its balance? What happens if that balance wobbles?

A photo of Earth taken from *Apollo 8* in 1969

Earth: Our Spot in Space

Only a few astronauts had seen what Earth really looks like from a distance before 1968. That's when astronauts on *Apollo 8* sent back what's now a famous photo of our planet. The familiar "blue marble" is a gorgeous blue, brown, green, and white swirled globe against the pitch darkness of space.

Move in closer as you whisk through the clouds toward your continent. When you're back with your feet on the ground, you'll see the plants, animals, and people that are familiar to you—your environment. Your home.

You can read transcripts of the *Apollo 8* mission at this website. What do you think it was like to be one of the first humans to see Earth from space?

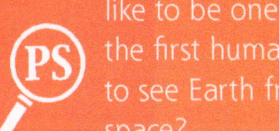 

🔍 NASA Apollo 8 transcript

What makes life on Earth possible? How can we live here and not, say, on the red planet of Mars? Why is Earth the only planet we know of where life exists?

It's all about our star—the sun—and the way our planet is perfectly placed in the solar system. Our global **ecosystem** all starts with the sun, which provides the light, energy, and heat that living things need to exist on Earth. The sun also activates our world's **water cycle**. In the water cycle, water **evaporates** from lakes, oceans, and rivers into water **vapor**. The water then **condenses** and falls again to Earth as rain or snow or ice, providing water to sustain life. All **organisms**—all life—depends on this water.

WORDS TO KNOW

Milky Way: the galaxy that contains our solar system.

ecosystem: an interdependent community of living and nonliving things and their environment.

bounty: a gift or generous supply of something.

species: a group of closely related and physically similar organisms.

water cycle: the process where the planet's water evaporates, condenses, and returns to Earth.

evaporate: to convert from liquid to vapor.

vapor: a substance suspended in the air as a gas, such as steam, mist, or fog.

condense: to change from a gas to a liquid.

organism: a living thing, such as a plant or animal.

DID YOU KNOW?

Rainforests offer Earth a living **bounty**. More than half of the world's insect, plant, and animal **species** live in the rainforests. The rainforests of Costa Rica alone have more than 1,300 species of butterflies.

7

PLANET EARTH

WORDS TO KNOW

natural resource: a material such as coal, timber, water, or land that is found in nature and is useful to humans.

food chain: a community of animals and plants where each is eaten by another higher up in the chain.

herbivore: an animal that eats only plants.

carnivore: an animal that eats only other animals.

predator: an animal or plant that kills and eats another animal.

kelp: large brown seaweed that grows in shallow ocean depths. It forms extensive forests that provide habitat for a wide variety of organisms.

habitat: a plant or animal's home, which supplies it with food, water, and shelter.

Our earth looks like a pretty rugged place. If you think about the power we can see in nature, such as hurricanes, earthquakes, and molten lava, it seems as though nothing could hurt our strong planet. But, if you look closer, you'll find it's a world that needs to maintain a careful balance in order to continue to grow and flourish.

Anywhere you look in the world, the environment is playing a balancing act between plants, animals, and **natural resources**, such as soil, energy, and water. Plants are the source for all the global **food chains**—for humans and all animals. The sun provides energy to plants, which become food for small **herbivores**. These are animals such as rabbits and mice. Then, larger **carnivores** eat the smaller animals.

The sun makes life on Earth possible

Seems simple, right? But what if part of that food chain were to be disrupted?

That's what has happened with sea otters. From the late 1700s into the early 1900s, people relentlessly hunted sea otters for their fur. As the sea otter population declined, the sea urchins—the sea otters' favorite food—didn't have any **predators** gobbling them up. So, the sea urchin population grew and ate up all the **kelp**— their favorite food.

credit: Laura Francis—National Oceanic and Atmospheric Administration (NOAA) Central Library

With less kelp in the sea, other animals, such as fish and small crabs, disappeared because they needed the **habitat** of the kelp beds as protective hiding places or as food sources. An entire mini-ecosystem was wiped out, all because the sea otters weren't around to keep the sea urchin population in balance.

The example of the sea otters shows just how delicate the earth's systems really are. Food chains such as this exist in every ecosystem. You can read more about food chains in Chapter 5.

This balance of our world and our environment is critical to life on the planet, and we need to understand how it all works. Think about it: What happens to kids on the playground if they're on a seesaw and one rider suddenly gets off? The balance is lost and it's a fast ride down! It's the same with our planet. If you change the balance or break up any of the systems that are in place, it'll throw off the rest of the systems.

PLANET EARTH

WORDS TO KNOW

biome: a large natural area with a distinctive climate, geology, set of water resources, and group of plants and animals that are adapted for life there.

diverse: a large variety.

geology: the rocks, minerals, and physical structure of an area.

adapt: to make a change to better survive in the environment.

deciduous: plants and trees that shed their leaves each year.

temperate: describes a climate or weather that is not extreme.

vegetation: all plant life in an area.

maize: corn.

fertile: land that is good for growing plants.

savanna: a dry, rolling grassland with scattered shrubs and trees.

abundant: a large amount.

BIOMES

One amazing fact about Earth is the way regions are different from each other. The landscape, animals, plants, and weather conditions vary dramatically all around the globe. A polar bear that thrives in the Arctic wouldn't last long in the hot Sahara Desert. And that sidewinder from the desert couldn't survive in the frozen tundra. Different **biomes** host **diverse** plants and animals that create their own balance.

A biome is a large natural area with a distinctive climate, **geology**, set of water resources, and group of plants and animals that are **adapted** for life there. Some examples of biomes include desert, ocean, mountain, tundra, forest, and grassland. Biomes and climates can be quite different within a relatively small area.

For example, along the southwest coast of South America is a **deciduous** forest biome where plants shed their leaves each year. Continuing east, you'll hit a mountainous biome, followed by **temperate** grassland, then a desert.

The animals and **vegetation** in any biome are not only dependent upon each other, but the people of the region also depend on them for food. A meal of broiled fish may be standard fare for someone living in Japan near the ocean, while over in grassy South Africa, a **maize**-based porridge might be a favorite food.

DID YOU KNOW? Scientists disagree how many biomes there are. Some scientists divide the world into five biomes, others 12, and some even believe there are more than 100 "eco-regions."

Biomes aren't permanent, either. Today, the Sahara Desert is about 4 million square miles of dry desert with an average of 3 inches of annual rainfall. But 10,000 years ago, the area wasn't a desert at all. It was a **fertile savanna** where elephants, giraffes, and other animals roamed, and plant life was **abundant**.

The Sahara Desert today

PLANET EARTH

WORDS TO KNOW

wetland: an area where the land is soaked with water. Wetlands are often important habitats for fish, plants, and wildlife.

lichen: a plant-like organism made of algae and fungus that grows on solid surfaces such as rocks or trees.

algae: a simple organism found in water that is like a plant but without roots, stems, or leaves.

fungi: mold, mildew, rust, and mushrooms. Plural of fungus.

aquatic: having to do with water.

plankton: microscopic plants and animals that float or drift in great numbers in bodies of water.

coniferous: plants and trees that do not shed their leaves each year.

food web: a network of connected food chains.

Closer to the present time, humans have transformed biomes. An example is in northwest Ohio in the United States. The Great Black Swamp was a **wetland** with vegetation such as ash, elm, and maple trees. In the late nineteenth century, though, the swamp was drained. Today, it's farmland.

One thing planet Earth has a lot of—air and water! In the next chapters, we'll take a closer look at these two important elements. We'll discover how much of an impact they have on us and we have on them.

ESSENTIAL QUESTION

What are some of the ways the environment where you live maintains its balance? What happens if that balance wobbles?

What does the tundra (seen below) have in common with the desert?

Know Your Biome Facts

Desert. One fifth of the earth's surface is made up of deserts. The desert is an extreme habitat. With very little rainfall and temperatures that can soar well beyond 120 degrees Fahrenheit (49 degrees Celsius), the desert is home to very few plants and animals. These are specially adapted to withstand high temperatures and dry conditions. For example, cactus and other plants have shallow roots to absorb any rain quickly. Desert dwellers, such as scorpions and kangaroo rats, are able to live on a minimal amount of water.

Tundra. In contrast to the desert's heat is the chill of the tundra biome, which is the coldest biome on our planet. Temperatures can drop to -50 degrees Fahrenheit (-46 degrees Celsius) and below. Although it might seem too cold for animals, the tundra is home to several species. Among them are caribou, seals, walrus, lemmings, and Arctic hares—and the biggest predator of the tundra, the polar bear. Plant life is less diverse—mostly mosses and some shrubs. **Lichens**, which are made of **algae** and **fungi**, are common.

Aquatic. The largest biome in the world, this includes all the water environments, from freshwater lakes to saltwater oceans. The **aquatic** biome covers about 70 percent of the earth's surface. The plants and animals living in an aquatic environment are diverse and plentiful, from the huge blue whale to the tiny **plankton** that it eats.

Forest. The forest biome has several subgroups, or divisions, including rainforests, **coniferous** forests (the largest land biome), and deciduous forests. Just as in the aquatic biome, plant and animal life flourish here. Along with the plant life, a wide range of animals live in forests to create huge, interconnected **food webs**.

Grassland. Not surprisingly, grasses rule in the grasslands. The land is covered with different kinds of grasses that grow tall and in abundance, with hardly any trees or shrubs in sight. Animals that live here are mostly herbivores. Some examples of herbivores are antelope, wild horses, and prairie dogs. But carnivores such as lions live here, too.

DID YOU KNOW? Penguins don't live just in the frozen Antarctic biome. They also live along the coast of South America, the Galapagos Islands, the southern coast of Africa, and along the coast of Australia.

Activity

MAKE YOUR OWN BACKYARD POND

Even if you have only a very small backyard, you can still create a pond to enjoy—just dig a smaller hole. If you have only patio or deck space, you can create an above-ground pond by using a watertight container. Create a pond and then see what kinds of creatures come to live in the new habitat!

> **Caution:** You must have permission from an adult to do this project.

▶ **Find a good location for your pond.** Consider whether the plants you want to grow need full or partial sunlight, or if overhanging trees will drop too many leaves into the pond during the autumn.

About the Projects

As you read this book and do the projects, be aware of the materials you use. For instance, you'll see many of the activities call for plastic, two-liter bottles. If you already get your drinks in this kind of bottle, a science or art project is a great way to recycle the container. You can also ask a neighbor or friend to save you one of their bottles. That way, you're not making a purchase you don't need, and materials aren't being used to make an extra bottle that you wouldn't have purchased otherwise. Same with other materials used for activities—be creative!

Some of the projects involve living creatures or plants. Handle everything with great care, and return them unharmed to the place where you found them so they can continue to be part of the environment. And be sure to stay safe when you're working near a body of water or using a knife or tool. Always have an adult help you!

Activity

❯ **Dig the space out for your pond.** If you want critters living in your pond, such as frogs or turtles, you may want to dig it out so there are two levels—a shallow rim around your pond, perhaps a foot or so deep, and a deeper level in the middle that is a couple of feet deep so your aquatic life will have a place to swim down to in order to escape predators. Be sure you're not digging an area that's larger than the plastic sheet you will use as a liner.

❯ **Spread your plastic sheet—an old shower curtain works well—over the area you've dug,** making sure it reaches all the way up the sides. Try to bring the sheet up over the edges of your pond. For now don't worry how it looks. You will cover it up with rocks and soil, then add plants later.

❯ **Pour sand, rocks, or other bottom cover over your plastic sheet.** This will weigh it down and prevent the sheet from floating up. Cover up the plastic sheet around the edges of your pond with large rocks or soil and grass seed.

❯ **Fill your pond.** If you're using water from the hose, wait at least a week for any chemicals to filter out of the water before adding any plants or animals.

❯ **Introduce plants to your pond** by setting some pots along the shallow edges. You can plant other things, such as water lilies, deeper. Talk to your local plant nursery or research online to learn about what plants are best for your area. Add water to your pond periodically to keep it full.

Think About It

What sort of wildlife comes to live in your pond? Do you have **amphibians** or **reptiles**? Insects and birds? Small **mammals**? What kinds of things grow in your pond? If you live in an area with changing seasons, what happens to your pond when it's colder or warmer? Keep track of your observations in your science journal.

WORDS TO KNOW

amphibian: an animal with moist skin that is born in water but lives on land. An amphibian changes its body temperature by moving to warmer or cooler places. Frogs, toads, newts, efts, and salamanders are amphibians.

reptile: an animal covered with scales that crawls on its belly or on short legs. A reptile changes its body temperature by moving to warmer or cooler places. Snakes, turtles, lizards, alligators, and crocodiles are reptiles.

mammal: a type of animal, such as a human, dog, or cat. Mammals are born live, feed milk to their young, and usually have hair or fur covering most of their skin.

Activity

MAKE YOUR OWN TULLGREN FUNNEL

The ground you walk on is more complex than you may realize. Not only is the geology fascinating, but the ground is also home to animals you probably don't even know are there. Scientists who want to study the very small creatures who live in the soil and **leaf litter** use a Berlese-Tullgren funnel, named after the scientists who created it more than 100 years ago. You can uncover some of these incredible little critters when you create your own funnel.

▶ **Wrap black construction paper around a wide-mouthed jar** so it covers the outside. Secure it with tape.

▶ **Cut a small piece of mesh, such as from an old window screen,** and place it in the bottom of a funnel so it blocks the hole. Set the funnel into the mouth of the jar. The screen will prevent your soil or leaf litter from falling into your jar.

▶ **Fill the funnel with fresh soil.** If you're using leaf litter, use the leaf litter that's at the very bottom of the pile you find. Or try setting up a couple of different Tullgren funnels, using soil in one and leaf litter from different layers or from different locations in another.

▶ **Set up a desk lamp so that it shines down directly on the soil or leaf litter in the funnel,** but not so close that it burns it.

▶ **Wait about an hour.** As the tiny creatures in the soil or leaf litter try to move away from the light and heat, they'll move downward through the funnel and fall into your jar.

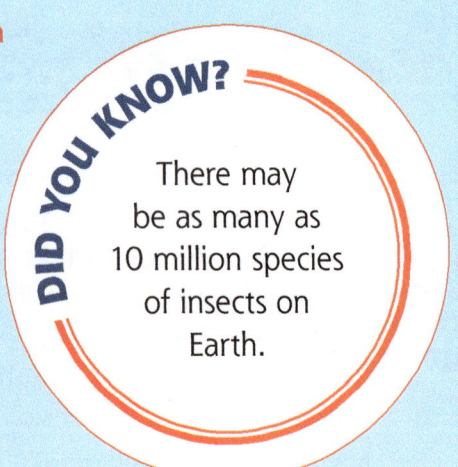

DID YOU KNOW? There may be as many as 10 million species of insects on Earth.

16

Activity

> **After the time is up, take the construction paper off the jar.** Examine the critters you've found using a magnifying glass or microscope. You may find critters such as mites, nematodes (microscopic worms), earthworms, and beetles. The larger creatures will be on the screen in the bottom of the funnel, since they won't fit through the holes in the screen.

> **After you've examined what you've found,** be sure to release everything back to the soil.

Think About It

All the creatures you find in soil and leaf litter are important to the ecosystem because they are often the beginning of food chains. As plants and animals **decay**, these critters consume the **organic** matter directly or they consume the **bacteria** and fungi that break down plant and animal matter. Then, these tiny creatures are eaten by larger creatures that live in the soil, which are then consumed by larger insects or birds.

WORDS TO KNOW

leaf litter: fallen leaves and other dead plant material that is starting to break down.

decay: to break down and rot.

organic: something that is or was living, such as wood, paper, grass, insects, and animals.

bacteria: tiny organisms found in soil, water, plants, and animals that are sometimes helpful and sometimes harmful.

Activity

WHOLE WORLD GRANOLA

Reflect the diversity of life on Earth in a yummy snack!

Ingredients

½ cup dry milk
5 cups dry oatmeal
1 teaspoon cinnamon
pinch of salt
⅓ cup honey
¾ cup brown sugar
⅓ cup vegetable oil

Whole-world add-ins:
chocolate, raisins,
coconut, dates,
Brazil nuts, dried pineapple,
almonds, sunflower seeds,
sesame seeds, pecans,
dried cranberries

▶ **Mix together the first four ingredients in a large baking dish.** Mix in 2 cups of whole-world add-ins—except for chocolate chips, pineapple, or raisins, if you're using them. These can be added after baking, so they don't melt or get too hard.

▶ **Have an adult help you with the stove.** In the saucepan, mix together the honey, brown sugar, and oil. Heat over medium heat until the sugar dissolves, stirring constantly to make sure it doesn't burn.

▶ **Pour the sugar mixture over the oat mixture and combine well.** Be sure to coat as much of the dry mix as possible. Bake at 375 degrees Fahrenheit for 10 minutes, or until the granola is crunchy enough for your taste.

▶ **Let the granola cool in the pan before breaking it into chunks and mixing in the rest of the add-ins** (the chocolate chips, dried pineapple, and raisins). Store in an airtight container.

Try This!

Research the regions your ingredients came from. On a world map, mark the countries you just took a bite of.

Chapter 2

THE PLANET OF
AIR AND WATER

Planet Earth is unique for many reasons, including our atmosphere and our abundance of water. These are what separate Earth from all other planets in the solar system. Both of these things are critical for life. Without them, humans, animals, plants, microbes—none of these would exist!

Our atmosphere and our water systems work together in a complex way to provide the resources we need to exist. Has there been a storm where you live lately? The weather is the atmosphere in action! Rain, snow, sleet, hail, and wind are all signs that air and water are on the move. It's these continuous cycles that keep our planet comfortable for all kinds of diverse species. Let's take a closer look!

ESSENTIAL QUESTION

How are air and water part of the same system?

PLANET EARTH

WORDS TO KNOW

microbe: a tiny living or nonliving thing. Another word for microorganism.

oxygen: the most abundant element on Earth, found in the air and in the water.

ultraviolet (UV): invisible light radiated from the sun.

element: a substance that is made of one type of atom, such as iron, carbon, or oxygen.

carbon dioxide: a gas formed by the burning of fossil fuels, the rotting of plants and animals, and the breathing out of animals, including humans.

anaerobic: without oxygen. The opposite of aerobic, with oxygen.

stomata: tiny pores on the outside of leaves that allow gases and water vapor to pass in and out.

gills: filter-like structures that let an organism get oxygen out of the water to breathe.

WELCOME TO THE ATMOSPHERE

Air surrounds us here on Earth. You can't see it or smell it, but Earth's atmosphere, the mixture of gases that blanket the globe, is a vital part of our environment. It's critical to life on our planet.

Not only does the atmosphere supply the **oxygen** that we need to breathe, but it protects us from the sun's **ultraviolet (UV)** rays. And it also soaks up most of the sun's incredible heat so the temperatures on the surface of the Earth stay in a range that can sustain life. The lowest level of the atmosphere is where our weather occurs. Weather is part of the water cycle that brings us the water we need.

What is air really? If you said oxygen, you're partly right. Air is made up of a mixture of gases, and oxygen is one of them.

> **DID YOU KNOW?** People sometimes think air is mostly oxygen—but it's not. Most of the air we breathe, 78 percent, is actually nitrogen, and only 21 percent is oxygen.

A scientist named Joseph Priestley discovered the elements of air. You can see the apparatus he used in his investigation at this website. Can you figure out how this works? Do some research at the library or online if you need some help.

🔎 Joseph Priestley experiments

The Planet of Air and Water

Air is also made of nitrogen, small amounts of **carbon dioxide**, a gas called argon, and some other trace gases. Pretty much all organisms need oxygen to survive on Earth. The few organisms that don't need oxygen are called **anaerobic**. They live in oxygen-free places such as the hot volcano vents in the ocean.

The plants that surround you—trees, houseplants, grass, bushes—all "breathe" air just as animals do.

Instead of lungs, though, plants use microscopic openings on their leaves to take in gases and release moisture and oxygen. These tiny openings are called **stomata**. A plant can close its stomata to retain moisture at night or if conditions are too dry.

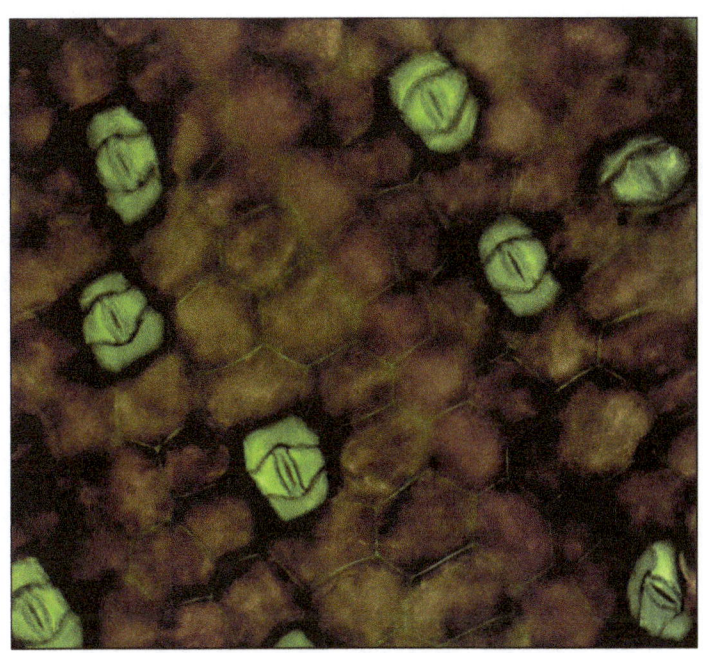

A close-up of the stomata on a leaf

Fish Need Air, Too

Fish, surrounded by water, need air to breathe, too. Oxygen is dissolved in water, and fish get the oxygen they need through their **gills**. A fish opens its mouth and takes in water. When the fish closes its mouth, the water passes over its gills, which contain tiny blood vessels that can extract the oxygen from the water—up to 85 percent of the available oxygen—and send it into the fish's bloodstream.

PLANET EARTH

WORDS TO KNOW

chlorophyll: a pigment that makes plants green, used in photosynthesis to capture light energy.

glucose: a type of sugar a plant makes for food.

photosynthesis: the process plants use to turn sunlight, carbon dioxide, and water into food.

troposphere: the lowest part of the earth's atmosphere, where most weather occurs.

stratosphere: the middle region of the atmosphere, where the ozone layer is.

ozone: a gas that is a major air pollutant in the lower atmosphere but a beneficial part of the middle atmosphere. The ozone layer blocks most of the sun's ultraviolet radiation.

radiation: the process of energy from light or sound moving from its source, such as the sun, radiating outward.

beneficial: having good or helpful results.

mesosphere: the atmosphere above the stratosphere but below the thermosphere.

meteor: a streak of light produced when a small particle from outer space enters the earth's atmosphere.

thermosphere: the thickest part of the atmosphere, rising more than 300 miles above the surface of Earth.

exosphere: a very thin layer of gas surrounding a planet.

molecule: a group of atoms bound together. Molecules combine to form matter.

atom: the smallest particle of matter in the universe that makes up everything, like tiny building blocks or grains of sand.

Plants absorb the carbon dioxide in the air through the stomata. Along with **chlorophyll**, the green substance in their leaves, plants use the carbon dioxide to make **glucose**, which provides energy that the plant needs to live. When sunlight reaches the plant's leaves, it starts the **photosynthesis** process, and the oxygen that is left over from the glucose-making process is released into the air.

DID YOU KNOW?

Plants actually "breathe" out carbon dioxide, just like we do. But they also produce oxygen after photosynthesis, which is one reason they're so important to the environment.

LOOK AT THE LAYERS

Earth's atmosphere is categorized in these layers.

- **Troposphere.** This is the layer that's at our level—starting from the ground up. It reaches up about 12 miles high, and it's thicker at some parts of the globe than others. Airplanes fly in this layer of the atmosphere, and it's where most of Earth's weather happens, too. The higher up you go, the colder it gets.

- **Stratosphere**. This layer rises up from the troposphere to a height of around 30 miles. Unlike the troposphere, it gets hotter in the stratosphere the higher up you go. No weather is in the stratosphere and commercial airplanes can't fly this high, but weather balloons do go up here. **Ozone**, which is a gas created by UV **radiation** from the sun interacting with oxygen, is in the stratosphere. Ozone helps protect Earth from harmful UV radiation, so it is **beneficial** here.

- **Mesosphere**. The mesosphere rises up about 56 miles above the earth's surface. Together with the stratosphere, it's considered the "middle atmosphere." Many **meteors** burn up when they enter the mesosphere. We see them as shooting stars.

- **Thermosphere**. The thickest part of the atmosphere, the thermosphere rises more than 300 miles above the surface of Earth. The space shuttle orbits in the thermosphere.

- **Exosphere**. The last layer of the atmosphere, the exosphere is where any gases begin to thin and the **molecules** separate and drift into space.

> **Ozone gets a lot of attention, usually in a negative way. But ozone is helpful. At least, ozone is helpful when it's where it belongs, which is up in the stratosphere.**

We breathe oxygen made up of two oxygen **atoms**. Ozone is a gas made up of three oxygen atoms. It forms a kind of shield against the sun's harmful ultraviolet rays. But when harmful gases from aerosol cans or air conditioners rise up to the ozone layer, they make the ozone weaker, so it can't do its job as well.

credit: NOAA

PLANET EARTH

WORDS TO KNOW

suburban: having to do with living areas at the edges of cities.

dense: tightly packed.

rural: areas in the countryside.

rotation: a turn all the way around.

Santa Ana winds: Southern California winds that occur when air changes temperature while moving over mountains.

equator: the imaginary line around the planet halfway between the North and South Poles.

mid-latitudes: the areas halfway between the equator and the North and South Poles.

trade winds: winds that blow almost continually toward the equator from the northeast north of the equator and from the southeast south of the equator.

Tropospheric ozone is down here at our level. It's caused by pollution from things such as car exhaust. When we inhale ozone, it's bad for our lungs. Ozone usually forms when it's hot, for example, on hot afternoons in the summer. And although it's usually found in urban and **suburban** settings where the population is **dense**, wind can carry it far into **rural** areas.

BLOWING IN THE WIND

We can't usually see air, but we can see the work air does when it's moving, whether it's gently rustling the leaves on the trees or whipping up desert sands into an intense sandstorm. Wind is the result of moving air masses in the lower levels of the atmosphere and of the **rotation** of Earth.

When the sun shines down on Earth, land masses absorb heat, while areas of water reflect most of it back. As air warms, it gets lighter and rises. Any cool air mass nearby will rush in to fill that space because cold air is denser and heavier than warm air. When the air moves in this way, it creates wind.

Wind doesn't always blow in one direction. Along coastlines, the wind blows from sea to shore, because the land heats up quickly during the day, heating the air above it But at night, the water retains heat longer than land, so the winds change direction and blow from the land to sea.

DID YOU KNOW? The strongest "regular" surface wind ever recorded was 231 miles per hour at the top of Mount Washington in New Hampshire. Tornadoes have been known to blow even stronger.

The Planet of Air and Water

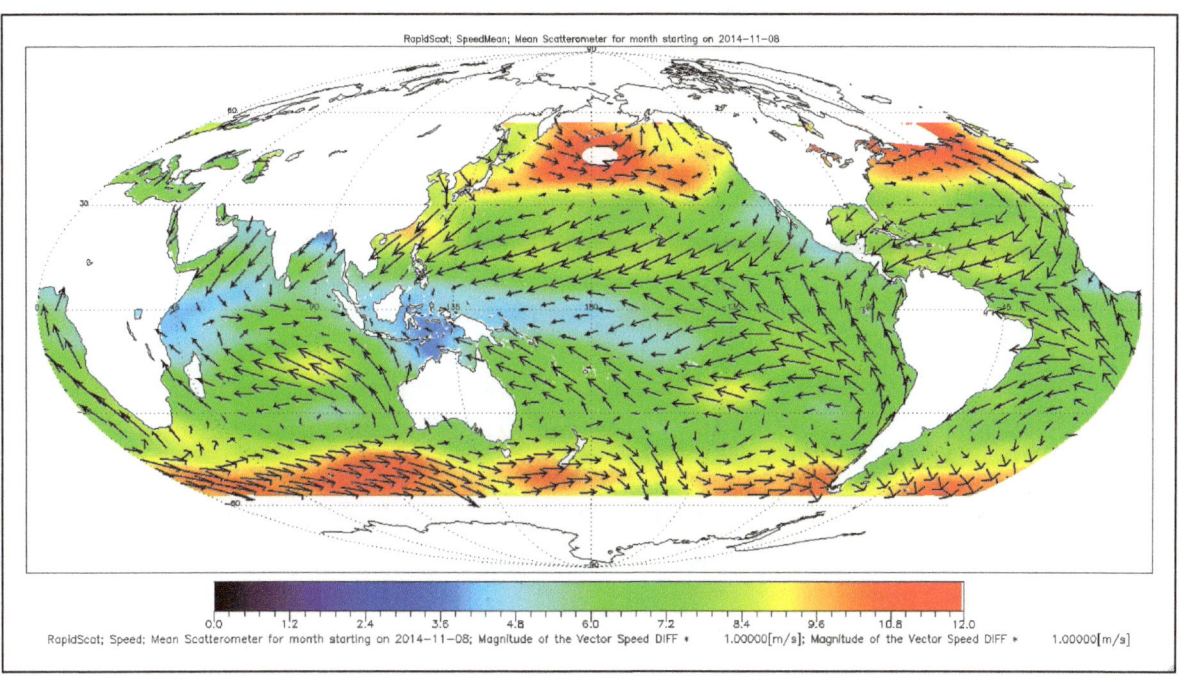

The monthly average winds for November 2014
credit: NASA/JPL-Caltech

While winds can change according to different weather patterns, some are predictable depending on the seasons of the year. People in southern California, for example, are familiar with the hot **Santa Ana winds** that stir up in late summer.

Wind patterns that blow from east to west also form around the **equator**.

The winds blow west to east in the **mid-latitudes**, and east to west again near the North and South Poles. These winds are called **trade winds**, because back in the times of merchant ships with sails, these winds helped move ships across the ocean, and they defined the routes that ships traveled.

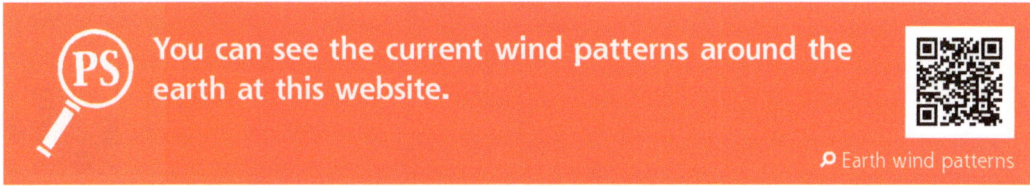

PLANET EARTH

WORDS TO KNOW

current: the steady flow of water or air in one direction.

El Niño: unusually warm ocean conditions occurring every few years along the tropical west coast of South America. El Niño has dramatic affects on weather patterns around the world.

precipitation: the falling to Earth of rain, snow, or any form of water.

catastrophic: involving or causing large amounts of damage.

turbine: a machine with rotating blades that changes one type of energy to another, such as wind energy into electricity.

As the trade winds blow across the surface of the water, they set the water in motion, creating **currents** that affect climates around the globe. In some years, however—anywhere from two to 10 years apart—the trade winds don't blow. The lack of trade winds is called **El Niño**, and it has an impact on the entire earth.

When the trade winds from South America stop, cool water is no longer pushed west and the water warms up. The water warms up all the way up the west coast of the Americas, even as far as Washington state. The result? Air masses all over the globe are affected, and abnormal weather patterns result.

Spanish fishermen in South America noticed the warmer waters arriving around Christmas time, and named them "El Niño." This means "the little boy" in Spanish, and refers to the birth of Christ.

Ocean Currents

Just as winds blow with relative consistency around the globe, regular ocean currents move water of different temperatures around the earth. Warm currents, or water that flows from warmer areas, such as the equator, bring higher temperatures and more **precipitation** to an area. The reverse is true of colder currents. In addition, strong winds blowing across the surface of the ocean have an impact on the currents, steering them in the direction of the wind. The rotation of Earth also is responsible for currents.

 You can see real-time ocean currents and patterns at this website.

🔎 current marine data

WIND POWER

In some cases, the force of the wind can be **catastrophic**—just think of a hurricane. However, the force can also be harnessed to create a clean energy source.

Using a **turbine**, wind power can be converted to energy. Wind turns the blades of the turbine, which turn a central drive shaft inside the turbine. A gear box transfers the relatively slow speed of the shaft into a much higher speed, and a generator transforms that spinning energy into electrical energy.

DID YOU KNOW? Turbines need an average wind speed of only 14 miles per hour to convert wind energy to electricity.

Wind turbines such as these convert wind into energy.

PLANET EARTH

> **WORDS TO KNOW**
>
> **cell:** the basic building block of all living organisms.
>
> **buoyant:** light and floating.
>
> **permeable:** a substance that liquid (or gas) can flow through.
>
> **water table:** the underground water supply for the planet.

As people continue to look for better ways to produce energy, wind power use continues to climb every year. Energy produced by burning fossil fuels can contribute to an overload of carbon dioxide in the atmosphere. Energy from the wind doesn't require much burning of fossil fuels. As of 2018, Denmark is the world leader in wind power—20 percent of electricity in Denmark is generated by the wind.

WATER, WATER EVERYWHERE

Water is essential to all life on Earth. Your body needs water. In fact, your brain alone is about 70 percent water. Your **cells**, and the cells of every living thing, need water to function and survive.

Fortunately, water makes up almost 71 percent of the entire Earth. Most of this is salt water, though, and less than 3 percent of Earth's water is fresh water. And, here's something interesting: The water that's on Earth today, in all forms—salt water, fresh water, rain, ponds, even someone's tears—is the same water that's been around since Earth was formed.

Water can be frozen in the tundra, stored inside a cactus in the desert, or guzzled down after a soccer game, but it always finds its way back into the water cycle eventually, to be used for something else for another million years. That sip of water you just took could have contained molecules that also quenched a T-Rex's thirst millions of years ago!

 Bernard Palissy was a French artist and author who is credited with coming up with the idea of a water cycle. His art often reflected water images. **You can see two of his ceramic pieces at this website.**

🔎 Palissy oval basin

28

The Planet of Air and Water

The water cycle is a never-ending process in which water makes a loop through the environment.

Water falls from the clouds as precipitation, which can take different forms, such as rain, snow, or sleet. Most of this water falls into the oceans, because the surface area of Earth's oceans is almost 140 million square miles—it's hard to miss!

The water might also be absorbed into the ground or run off rocks or pavement into streams and rivers. Animals use the water in streams and rivers as their habitat or as drinking water as it flows back toward the ocean.

If water falls on land where plenty of plants grow, the plants use the water—and they need a lot of it—to grow and photosynthesize. Water that's not used by plants gets absorbed into the soil. It travels down a filtering process through layers of **permeable** rock, such as sandstone, to a "holding tank" deep underground, called the **water table**. The water flows through the water table slowly, eventually returning to the ocean.

DID YOU KNOW? Salt water is denser than fresh water—that's why it's easier to swim in the ocean than in a freshwater lake. The salt helps keep your body **buoyant**.

PLANET EARTH

> **WORDS TO KNOW**
>
> **glacier:** an enormous mass of frozen snow and ice that moves across the earth's surface.

The heat of the sun warms the water in lakes and oceans. As the water gets warmer, the surface water starts evaporating and becomes water vapor. It rises into cooler air, where it condenses and eventually returns to Earth as precipitation. Then, the cycle begins again.

The driving force behind all of these cycles that provide the water and gases all organisms need to live is the sun! In the next chapter, we'll take a look at what exactly the sun is and why we can't exist without it.

> **ESSENTIAL QUESTION**
>
> How are air and water part of the same system?

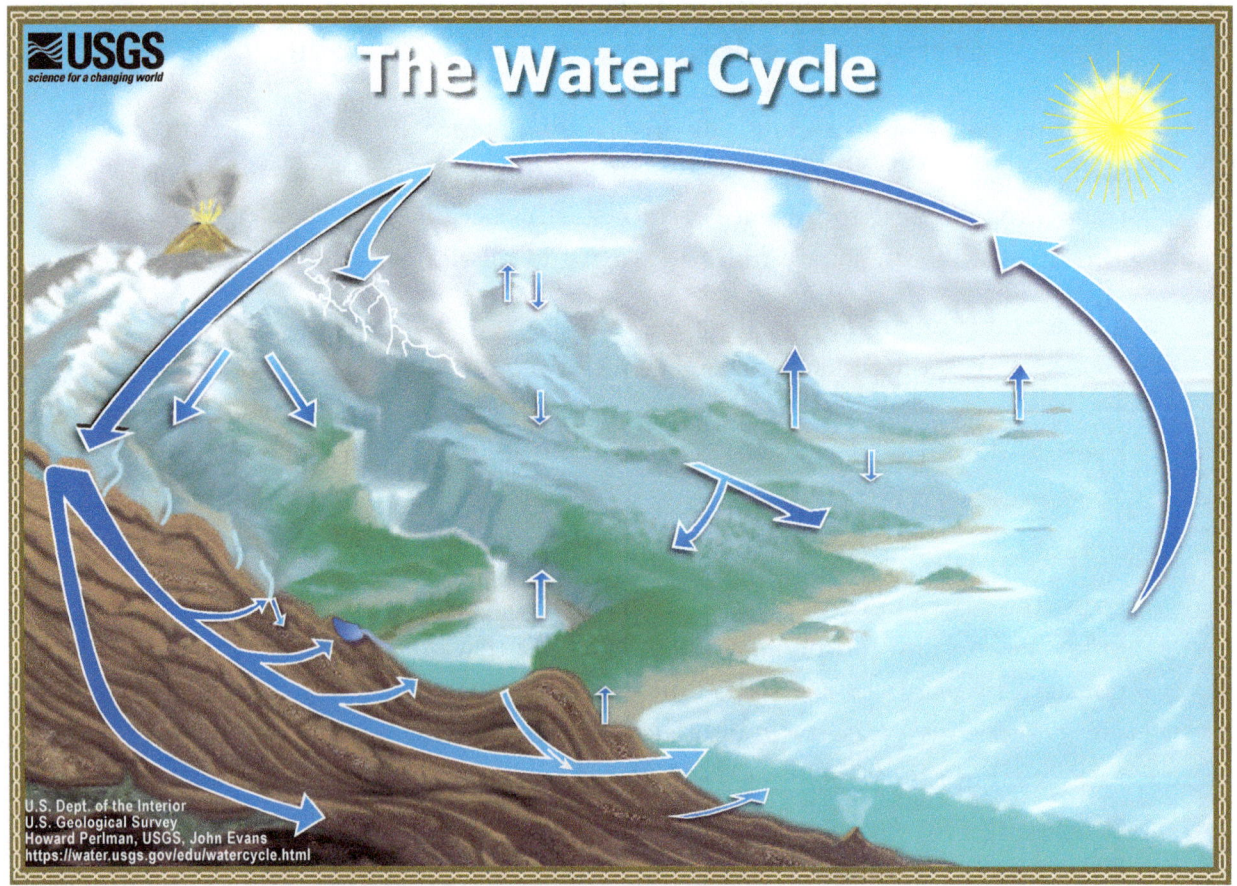

30

Glaciers

About 75 percent of the earth's freshwater is trapped in **glaciers**. These are mostly in Greenland and Antarctica, but also in Alaska and on very high mountain peaks around the world. If all the glaciers were to melt, ocean levels would rise more than 200 feet!

Glaciers are constantly moving—advancing and retreating as the ice melts and then freezes again. They grind huge, smooth, U-shaped valleys in the earth as they slowly scrape over the ground, like a frozen river flowing. Even after a glacier has long gone, the changes on the landscape remain in the form of valleys and hills. Although glaciers usually move slowly—some move about 4 inches a day—sometimes a glacier "surges." When this happens, a glacier can move anywhere between 10 to 100 times faster than its usual rate.

Scientists are studying retreating glaciers as indicators of the health of our global climate. Many believe that global warming is causing the glaciers to melt at a much faster speed than in the past.

These photos of Muir Glacier in Alaska show how much the glacier has shrunk in 70 years.

credit: NASA

Activity

WATCH PLANTS BREATHE

This experiment will help you see that plants really do breathe. Even though they don't have lungs, plants release gases into the air, just like we do.

❱ **Using a plant with runners**—such as a spider plant—carefully insert a runner into the bottom of a test tube or drinking glass. Try to find a runner that's small enough so it doesn't touch the end of the test tube or the top of the glass.

❱ **Put two or three lumps of modeling clay around the rim of the test tube.** This will help it stick in the bottom of the bowl when you invert it.

❱ **Fill a large bowl with water,** and fill the test tube with water to the very top.

❱ **Carefully flip the test tube over so that no water escapes and submerge it in the bowl of water.** Stick it to the bottom of the bowl using the modeling clay. If you're having trouble keeping water in the test tube when you flip it, try holding a plastic card (such as an old credit card) tightly over the top of the tube, then flipping the tube and sliding the card off once the tube is underwater.

❱ **Set the plant and the bowl with the test tube in direct sunlight and wait a couple of hours.** When you return, record your observations in your science notebook. What do you see? Why do you think that happened?

What's Happening?

Do you see a pocket of gas at the top of the tube? That's where the plant has released oxygen and forced the water out from the tube. The plant leaf has released oxygen after its photosynthesis and **displaced** the water from the tube. If you wait longer, you can see how the plant produces more oxygen, which it normally releases into the environment, unseen.

WORDS TO KNOW

displace: to cause something to move from its usual or proper place.

Activity

MAKE YOUR OWN GIANT AIR BLASTER

Feel how strong air can be when you make this giant air blaster. Stack up some paper cups and send them flying with the blaster.

Caution: Ask an adult to help you cut a hole in the bucket.

▶ **Using wire snips, cut a 2-inch hole** in the middle of the bottom of a 15-gallon bucket. This will be your blaster.

▶ **Stretch a piece of thick plastic, such as an old shower curtain,** tightly over the top of the bucket, and secure it with a bungee cord.

▶ **To fire your blaster, hold it sideways with the hole pointing at whatever you want to blast.** Sharply rap the plastic with your fist or a stick. What happens? How large a force can you create with the air?

It can be confusing to think of wind becoming energy. How do spinning blades create something that will charge your laptop or phone? **To learn how this works, watch the video at this website.** What are some of the pros and cons of wind energy? Do you think we'll use more wind energy in the future?

🔍 **PS**

🔎 Khan Academy wind energy

What's Happening?

The movement of the air in the bucket, forced quickly through the smaller hole, will create a rushing gust of "wind." If you can use the wind to knock over light items, imagine what people could do if they developed more ways of harnessing wind energy!

33

Activity

IS IT ACIDIC?

Every liquid, including water, is either **acidic** or **alkaline**. A liquid's **pH** value indicates its acidity or alkalinity. Distilled water is an exception. It has a neutral pH, which means it's neither acidic nor alkaline. You can rank liquids on a scale from the most acidic to the most alkaline, using pH test paper, or litmus paper.

> **Caution:** Ask an adult to help you obtain different liquid samples.

▶ **Collect water samples from different sources,** such as a pond, bottled water, rainwater, a street puddle, tap water, and more. Then, use your imagination to find a lot of different samples of liquids. For example, you can try distilled water, dissolved baking soda, vinegar, soapy water, milk, and lemon juice.

▶ **Start a scientific method worksheet and create a chart in you science journal for comparing liquid samples.** Test the pH of each sample to check its acidity. Acids turn pH paper red—compare the shade of color on your paper with the indicator that came with the package of pH paper. Record your findings.

▶ **Which of your samples were most acidic?** Least acidic, or alkaline? Do you see a pattern to the results? Did any of them surprise you?

Try This!

If you collect water from outside, run each sample through a coffee filter into a container. Look at what was in the water with a microscope or magnifying glass.

Why is it important to know if a substance is acidic or alkaline? Some organisms thrive in acidic environments, while others suffer. Plus, knowing the pH of a liquid can also help you decide if it makes a good household cleaner!

WORDS TO KNOW

acidic: describes a substance that is low on the pH scale and loses hydrogen in water. Examples of acidic substances include lemon juice and vinegar.

alkaline: describes a substance that is high on the pH scale and gains hydrogen in water. Examples of basic substances include soap, baking soda, and ammonia.

pH: a measure of acidity or alkalinity, on a scale from 0 (most acidic) to 14 (most alkaline).

Activity

MAKE YOUR OWN MINIATURE WATER CYCLE

You can see the water cycle in action by using the sun to warm up a bowl of water. The water will evaporate, and the plastic wrap will catch the water vapor. As more water vapor gathers, it will condense and "rain" back into your bowl. Take a look!

> **Fill a bowl with a couple inches of water.** Stretch plastic wrap over the top of the bowl and secure it around the opening with rubber bands. Set a stone in the middle of the wrap. Place the bowl in direct sunlight.

> **What do you see collecting on the plastic wrap?** This is evaporating water condensing back into liquid form. The stone you put on top will make a low point for the water to collect on when it condenses. If you wait, the droplets will become so heavy they'll "rain" back down into the bowl.

DID YOU KNOW? The Dead Sea has such a high concentration of salt that it's more than eight times saltier than the ocean. It's so salty because it's land-locked, which means no rivers or streams flow from the Dead Sea. The water can't go anywhere except through evaporation, leaving all that salt behind. It's so dense you can't really swim in the Dead Sea. You just bob like a cork.

Try This!

Try the experiment again with salt water. You can get it right from the ocean if you're near a beach, or just mix in table salt. The "rain" that falls will not be salty. It will be fresh water because the salt stays behind in the original water. Take some of the salt water and put it on a plate outside in direct sunlight. When the water evaporates, what do you see?

OUR STAR, THE SUN

Every morning, you can count on it. In virtually every location around the globe, the sun rises in the east. And every evening, it sets in the west. It's one of Earth's most reliable and familiar rhythms, and it has been since Earth was formed.

For thousands of years, people have worshipped the sun as it followed its familiar path across the sky, bringing life and light to Earth. Farmers depend on it for their crops. Plants need it for photosynthesis. And for some people, sunrises and sunsets are the stuff of songs and poems.

ESSENTIAL QUESTION

How do you think life on Earth would be different if we were closer to the sun? What if we were farther away?

Our Star, the Sun

Our star, the sun, is the largest **celestial body** in our solar system. About a million Earths would fit inside the sun. And it's the only resident in our solar system that can produce its own energy. But scientists say that in comparison to other stars in the universe, the sun isn't really that big.

> **WORDS TO KNOW**
>
> **celestial body:** a star, planet, moon, or other object in space.
>
> **yellow dwarf:** a small star, such as our own sun.

The sun is called a **yellow dwarf** and is about one-sixth the size of a giant star. But it's plenty hot for life on Earth. Even though the earth is about 93 million miles away from the sun, in some places on Earth, the temperature rises to more than 150 degrees Fahrenheit (66 degrees Celsius) from the sun's rays. And think about this—Earth is only receiving two-billionths of the sun's rays!

credit: NASA

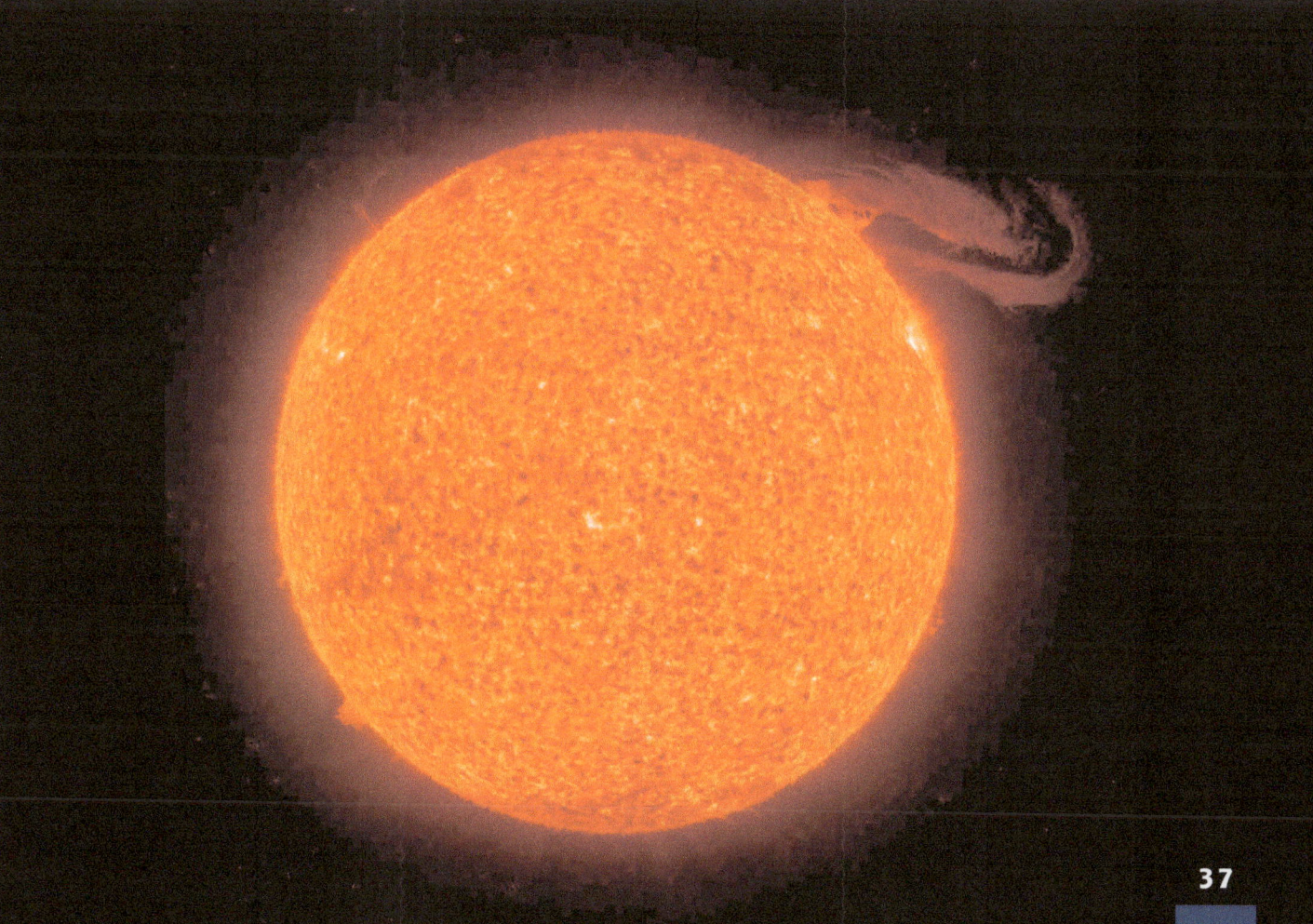

PLANET EARTH

> **WORDS TO KNOW**
>
> **by-product:** an extra and sometimes unexpected or unintended result of an action or process.
>
> **ectothermic:** cold-blooded. Describes animals such as snakes that have a body temperature that varies with the surrounding temperature.
>
> **vitamin D:** a vitamin that is important for bones and teeth. It is found in egg yolks and milk, and it can be produced in the body from sunlight.
>
> **solar power:** energy from the sun converted to electricity.
>
> **fossil:** the remains of any organism, including animals and plants, that have been preserved in rock.

LIVING CREATURES AND THE SUN

Plants depend on the sun for photosynthesis. The sun's rays give the chlorophyll inside the plant's cells the energy they need to convert water and carbon dioxide to glucose. Plants need glucose for energy, and when they make glucose, they also make oxygen, which is given off as a **by-product**.

The energy stored inside the plant's cells gets transferred to animals when the animals consume the plants. Living creatures use this energy to grow, build and repair cells, and perform other necessary life functions.

Ectothermic reptiles need the sun to warm their bodies so they can digest food and have energy to move around. And humans need the sun for our bodies to make **vitamin D**.

As you can see, the sun is a critical part of life on Earth.

credit: Zappy's Technology Solutions (CC BY 2.0)

SOLAR POWER

The sun is the main energy producer on our planet. Not only as **solar power** or in the heating of the soil and water, but also in less direct ways. When the sun heats air masses, the air masses begin to move, which creates wind power.

Our Star, the Sun

When the sun heats the oceans, water evaporates, enters the water cycle, condenses, and falls to Earth. The water in the water cycle feeds rivers and streams that can then generate energy.

The sun's energy from millions of years ago is helping us today, too, in the form of fossil fuels. Long ago, the energy passed from the sun to plants and animals and stayed in the plants and animals throughout their lifetimes. After those living creatures died and **fossilized** as millions of years passed, their remains became fossil fuels.

DID YOU KNOW? The surface of the sun itself is 10,000 degrees Fahrenheit (5,538 degrees Celsius), but the core is a scorching 27 million degrees.

Learn about how solar panels work in this video. What are some of the challenges to using solar energy?

PBS solar power

PLANET EARTH

WORDS TO KNOW

renewable: something that isn't used up, that can be replaced.

axis: the imaginary line through the North and South Poles that the earth rotates around.

accurate: true, correct.

sundial: a tool that uses a shadow cast by the sun to determine the time.

curvature: the amount something is curved.

horizon: the line in the distance where the land or sea seems to meet the sky.

Fossil fuels are limited, though. When they're used up, they're gone for good. The good news is that solar power is **renewable**—it's constantly radiating down to the earth from the sun. Solar power can be used to heat businesses, homes, and pools. It can also generate electricity and even power solar cars.

USING THE SUN AS A TOOL

The sun is useful for other things, beyond providing energy for our lives. It can also help us tell time and find our way!

Although ancient people believed the sun revolved around the earth, we now know it's the other way around. Early explorers knew Earth's rotation on its **axis** and revolving path around the sun could give them a pretty **accurate** way of knowing the time and their location.

Our Star, the Sun

The earth is always in motion, turning on its axis and revolving in its orbit around the sun. Therefore, any shadows the sun casts upon the ground are going to change during the course of a day and throughout the year.

However, just poking a stick into the ground and examining its shadow can't give you the right time of day. The first **sundials** that were accurate used an angled piece of wood to account for the **curvature** of the earth. The shadow fell onto a chart that marked the hours of the day.

Even without a sundial, you can get a pretty good estimate of what time it is by using the sun's position. Here's how! Find the position of the sun. And be careful, all those warnings your mom has given about not looking directly at the sun are true.

> **Studies have found that your eyes can sustain damage from the sun, so be sure you never look at it directly.**

- If the sun is directly overhead, you're in luck—it's noon. If it's not noon yet, determine which direction is east by finding the **horizon** that the sun is closest to. If it's past noon, the sun will be closer to the western horizon.

The ruins of an ancient sundial in Armenia

PLANET EARTH

WORDS TO KNOW

wavelength: the spacing of sound or light waves.

tropics: the area near the equator.

- Divide the sky into four sections that are about equal. The halfway point should pass directly over your head. Note which of your four sections contains the sun.

- Each of your sections represents about a three-hour period. If the sun is in the first eastern section, it's between about 6 a.m. and 9 a.m. If it's in the first western section, it's between 3 p.m. and 6 p.m.

- You can get closer still by estimating how far along in the section the sun is. For example, halfway through the first eastern section it will be about 7:30 a.m.

DID YOU KNOW?

In the budding stages, the well-named sunflowers follow the sun's path during the day. In the morning, the flowers wake up facing the east, and turn their heads as the sun crosses the sky, until they end facing the west in the evening. Older plants usually remain facing east.

Where in the World?

You can also tell direction using the sun.

> Push a stick that's about 3 feet long into the ground. Pick an area that's relatively flat and free of debris so the stick will cast a good shadow on the ground.

> Mark the spot where the top of the stick's shadow falls. You can use a stone, twig, or whatever's handy. This spot will be your marker for west.

> Wait about 15 minutes, then mark the tip of the stick's shadow again (leave the original marker in place). This is your marker for east.

> When you draw a line connecting these two markers, you'll have a line that runs roughly east to west. If you position yourself with the east marker to your right and the west marker to the left, you'll be facing north, and south will be behind you.

ULTRAVIOLET RAYS

The sun sends different **wavelength**s of energy to Earth. Although the ozone in the stratosphere blocks much of the harmful light, it doesn't absorb it all. In fact, three types of UV rays are given off by the sun, and ozone absorbs only one type, UV-c, completely. Of the other two, the ozone absorbs UV-b only partially and doesn't absorb UV-a at all. These are the ultraviolet rays that can cause sunburn or even cancer.

UV-b levels are at their strongest around noon, when the sun's rays are coming down directly on the surface of the earth. When the rays are at an angle to the earth, in the early morning and late afternoon, the UV levels aren't as strong.

Also, you might be more likely to get a sunburn when you're vacationing in the **tropics**. Because the sun is positioned more directly overhead at the equator, and because the protective ozone is thinner over the tropics, the UV impact will be greater there.

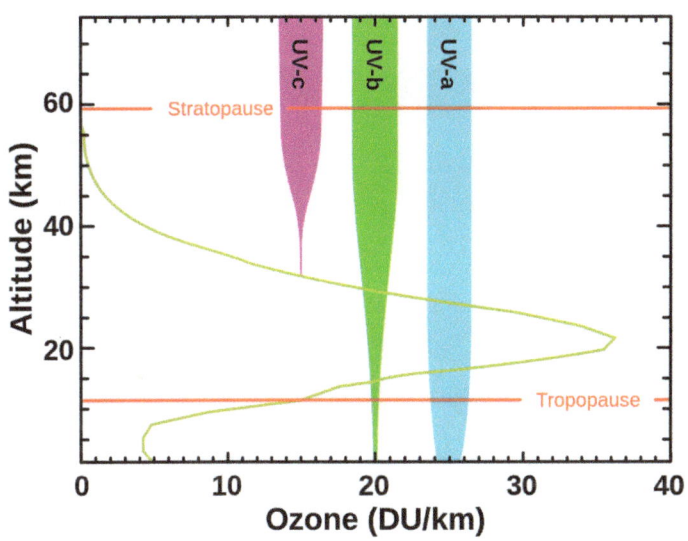

Check out how far each type of UV ray reached.
credit: NASA

Now that we know where the energy comes from for life to exist on Planet Earth, let's take a look at some of those different kinds of life and how they interact.

> **ESSENTIAL QUESTION**
>
> How do you think life on Earth would be different if we were closer to the sun? What if we were farther away?

Activity

MAKE YOUR OWN SOLAR-POWERED OVEN

Can you harness solar energy to cook? With this solar-powered oven you can. It'll take a little time (so be patient!) but if you direct the sun's rays carefully onto your food, it will actually cook.

❯ **Trace a square on the lid of a pizza box.** The square should be about an inch smaller than the lid.

❯ **Cut three sides of the square from the top of the pizza box.** Leave the fourth side (the side along the back) uncut to form a flap.

❯ **Open the box and cover the window you just cut with plastic wrap.** Try to tape it as tightly as possible so it's nice and taut.

❯ **Line the inside of the box, including the sides, with foil.** Also line the inside of the flap you cut with foil.

❯ **Cover the inside bottom of the box with black paper, fabric, or paint.** This will help absorb the sun's heat. Now you have a solar-powered oven!

Try This!

Test your oven! You can try using a graham cracker with a marshmallow on top or cheese on a cracker. Put your cooker in a spot where it will get direct sunlight. Angle the top of the solar cooker so that the sun reflects off your aluminum-foil-covered lid and into the cooker. Use a ruler or other object to prop the lid open at the perfect angle.

Check on your box in about half an hour to see how the food is progressing. Depending on the weather, it will take about twice the time to cook than in your regular oven indoors. Food will cook faster in the summer than in the winter. When your food is warm, enjoy!

Activity

MAKE YOUR OWN SOLAR CHIMNEY

You've probably heard that "heat rises," but have you ever seen that in action? With this simple project, you can harness the sun's solar power to generate heat to turn a pinwheel with its rising motion.

❯ **Create a chimney using three large tin cans** with both tops and bottoms removed. Tape them together so they don't topple.

❯ **Place two books on a flat surface in the sun,** a couple of inches apart, and place your chimney so it straddles the gap between the two.

❯ **Bend a paper clip into an arch,** and tape it over the top of your chimney.

❯ **Using an inverted thumb tack and a paper pinwheel** (you can find directions online on how to fold a square piece of paper into a pinwheel), mount your pinwheel on the top of the paper clip arch.

❯ **When you set the chimney in the sun,** wait to see how the heated air turns the pinwheel.

Think About It

What would happen if the chimney was flat on the ground instead of over the gap between the books? How would this affect the flow of air? Can you think of anything that you could use to heat the air in the cans faster? Caution: Never use anything that involves matches without the permission and supervision of an adult.

Activity

MAKE YOUR OWN HEAT TRANSFER PROJECT

There are different ways that solar energy transfers heat: conduction, radiation, and convection.

* **Conduction:** Heat flow from one part of a solid object to another object through direct contact (touching each other)

* **Radiation:** Heat energy transferred through movement of heat rays

* **Convection:** Heat flow through fluid or gas motion

▶ **Look around you to discover different ways of heat transfers** in your everyday life. If you've done the solar cooker experiment on page 44, do you know which method of heat transfer that used?

▶ **To experiment with conduction, think of a way to put one object that absorbs energy from the sun** in direct contact with another that would typically absorb energy at a slower rate. For instance, what could you put on top of an ice cube to make it melt faster through conduction?

▶ **For convection, how might air—a gas—moving change the temperature of something around it?** It doesn't have to be making something hotter. What is something you do to reduce the temperature of something by moving air across its surface? How about a mug of hot chocolate?

Think About It

What kind of heat transfer is happening when you cook pasta in a pot of boiling water? What kind of heat transfer does your heating system use to heat your home? What kind of heat transfer does the microwave use? Make a graph to discover the most common method of heat transfer happening in your house!

LIFE ON EARTH

Chapter 4

Life is everywhere on Earth. No matter which biome you're in—blistering desert, frigid tundra, steamy rainforest—life is there. Life exists even in the most extreme conditions on the planet, such as riding the smoking hydrothermal vents under the sea or buried deep inside a glacier. Life is one of the things that makes our planet unique in our solar system. All the different life forms on Earth are critical parts of our global environment.

ESSENTIAL QUESTION

What would happen if a species were suddenly gone from the earth?

Without any one of the three crucial ingredients of water, air, or sun, life as we know it would not exist on Earth. What's even more amazing is the diversity of life on our planet. All creatures aren't the same—far from it. Each has different defenses, habitats, diet, and communication.

PLANET EARTH

WORDS TO KNOW

hydrothermal vent: a crack in the sea floor where superheated fluid comes out.

classify: to put things in groups based on what they have in common.

kingdom: a broad division of living organisms.

virus: a non-living microbe that can cause disease.

vertebrate: an organism with a backbone or spinal column.

phylum chordata: a large group in the animal kingdom. It includes mammals, birds, fish, reptiles, and amphibians. These animals all have spinal cords.

class: a group of organisms with common attributes; a major category in grouping organisms.

homeotherm: an organism that can regulate its own body temperature.

CLASSIFICATION OF LIVING THINGS

People have always been fascinated by the process of **classifying** living things. Back in the 1700s, scientists relied on a system of two **kingdoms**: plants and animals. Later, that expanded to three, then to six kingdoms, and then to a multi-tiered tree as scientists found patterns among the vast differences in organisms.

As scientists learn more about unusual forms of life, such as **viruses** and other microscopic organisms, the kingdoms will undoubtedly change again. Why is it so complex?

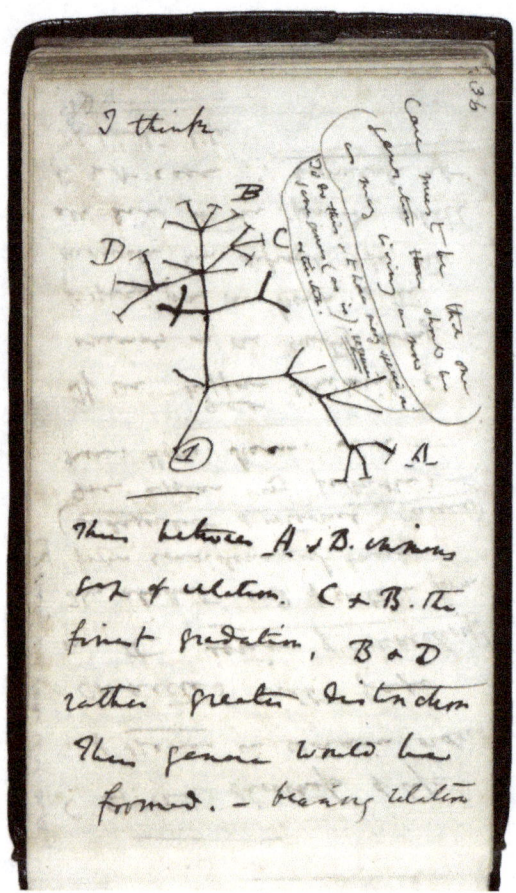

Scientist Charles Darwin (1809–1882) spent a lot of time classifying life. This is one of his early sketches.

Classification is similar to organizing everything in your house into a logical list. You'd have to find things that are similar by definition. But some things can cross into other defined groups. For example, a pair of red cotton socks could be grouped with "footwear," "cotton clothing," "red clothing," or "things that go in pairs."

48

How Living Things Are Classified

The classification of some organisms can be similar. Compare the classification of a coyote and a wolf. Because these two creatures are so similar, their classification is virtually the same, too, right down to the species. Your pet dog's classification is even closer to a wolf's. A dog's classification is C. lupus familiaris, which means the dog is a subspecies of the grey wolf (C. lupus). "Familiaris" means domestic—dogs are raised to be comfortable around humans.

Coyote: Animalia > Chordata > Mammalia > Carnivora > Canidae > Canis > C. latrans

Grey wolf: Animalia > Chordata > Mammalia > Carnivora > Canidae > Canis > C. lupus

Dog: Animalia > Chordata > Mammalia > Carnivora > Canidae > Canis > lupus familiaris

After classifying an organism into a kingdom, scientists still need to do more classifying. They break down groups of organisms further into subgroups, each getting more and more specific until a species is named.

FAMILIAR CLASSES

The organisms you're probably most familiar with are **vertebrates**, called **phylum chordata** by scientists. This large group of organisms is broken down into familiar **classes**.

One of those classes is mammals, which are **homeothermic** vertebrates that nurse their young and have hair in some form on their bodies—including humans! A few mammals do lay eggs, such as the platypus and echidna. Mammals are found on every continent on Earth.

PLANET EARTH

WORDS TO KNOW

symbiosis: a relationship between two different species of organisms in which each benefits from the other.

Birds are homeothermic vertebrates that have two legs and lay eggs. The variety of birds ranges from the 2½-inch bee hummingbird to the ostrich, which can be up to 9 feet tall. Birds, too, are found on every continent—even Antarctica.

Reptiles are ectothermic, meaning that they rely on an outside source of heat to stay warm. Most lay eggs. Because they need heat from their environment to help regulate their body temperature, they're not found in Antarctica, but they do live on every other continent. Amphibians are also ectothermic. Like reptiles, they need heat from their environment. Amphibians spend at least part of their lives in water.

You can find amphibians living on every continent except Antarctica.

Although scientists don't always agree about the classification of animals and plants, they do agree that all living creatures on Earth interact with each other and depend on each other for survival. Organisms are linked through the sharing of a habitat and through the food chain.

GETTING ALONG

Some organisms have a special way they interact with each other, known as **symbiosis**. Symbiosis occurs when two different species form a partnership with each other, often with mutually beneficial results—one helps the other, and the recipient returns the favor.

For example, the honeyguide bird eats beeswax and bee larvae, but it can't tear open a bee's nest. However, a ratel, which is a badger-like animal, can. The honeyguide spots a nest and flutters around the ratel's head, getting its attention and leading it to the nest. After the ratel has torn it open and eaten its fill of honey, the honeyguide can have its share, too. That's symbiosis!

DID YOU KNOW? No one knows for sure how many species of plants and animals there are in the world. Estimates are just that—educated guesses. Some scientists believe there are around 10 million species. Others estimate there are as many as 100 million!

Animals aren't the only ones that can form partnerships. The acacia plant is a thorny plant growing in hot regions. Ants make their home inside the large thorns and eat the plant's sweet secretions. The payback? When other insects or herbivores try to eat the acacia, the ants swarm from their homes and sting the intruder.

But the ants are smart. When bees come to pollinate the plant, the ants leave them alone, because the bees are helpful to the plant's survival.

 Watch a bee pollinating flowers in slow motion—a great example of two species relying on each other!

Smithsonian bumble bee

PLANET EARTH

WORDS TO KNOW

adaptation: the development of physical or behavioral changes to survive in an environment.

camouflage: the colors or patterns that allow a plant or animal to blend in with its environment.

minerals: nutrients found in rocks and soil that keep plants and animals healthy and growing. Salt and nitrogen are two minerals.

nutrients: substances that living things need to live and grow.

invasive species: a plant or animal species that enters an ecosystem and spreads quickly, harming the system's balance.

FOOD CHAINS AND WEBS

All animals on Earth have to eat other living things, whether it's plant life or animals. There's a pattern to what each animal eats. Let's take a look. A mouse eats some berries, and then a fox consumes the mouse. A fruit fly eats ripe fruit, a spider eats the fruit fly, and a bird eats spiders. These "straight line" eating patterns are called food chains.

When there's crossover between food chains, it's called a food web.

For example, a wasp could also eat the spider, or a hawk could consume a mouse. Life on Earth is tightly linked through food chains and webs.

All food chains on Earth start with the same thing—green plants, called the primary producers. From the blue-green algae in the oceans to tiny sprouts on land, food chains go up to the top predators, including raptors, crocodiles, wolves, and great white sharks.

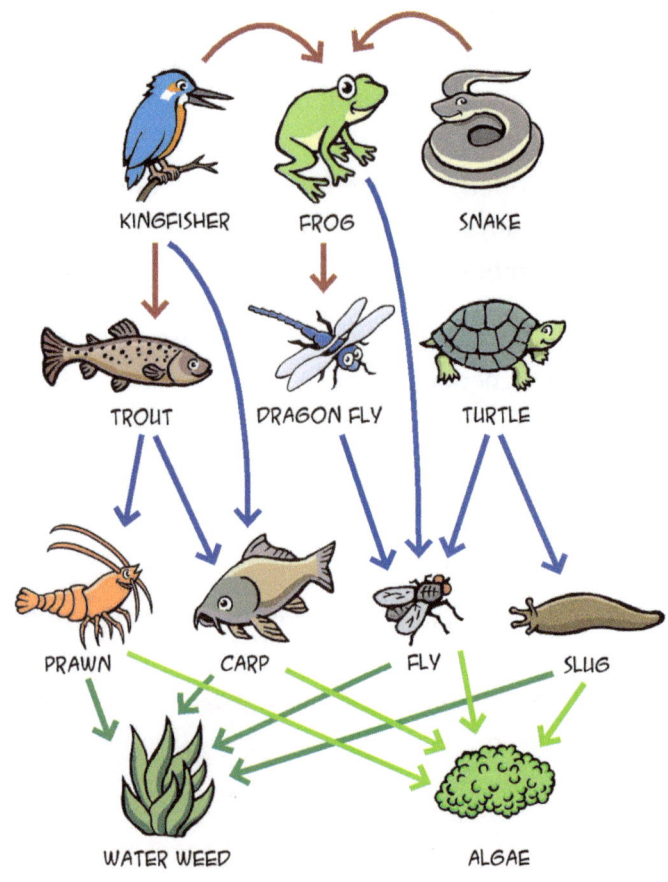

A food web of organisms that live on a pond or river

52

ADAPTATION

One of the many amazing aspects of life on Earth is how it has adapted to survive even the most extreme conditions. Some animals haven't changed for millions of years—such as the crocodile, which has remained virtually the same since the age of the dinosaurs. But other animals have adapted through time, developing coat or skin patterns to blend in with their environments. Animals such as the Arctic hare take on this **adaptation** seasonally, growing a white coat for **camouflage** in the snow in winter and a reddish-brown coat in the summer.

Some plants have unique adaptations, too. Have you ever spent time watching a carnivorous plant? The Venus flytrap grows in coastal North and South Carolina in the United States. Like other plants, it needs **minerals** from the soil. But conditions in the coastal soil weren't sufficient to provide these. So, the flytrap developed its unique method of catching and absorbing insects to provide the **nutrients** it needs.

Now that we've taken a good look at our amazing planet, let's think more about that environmental balance. How is the planet suffering, why is it suffering, and what can you do about it? We'll learn more in the next chapter.

> **ESSENTIAL QUESTION**
>
> What would happen if a species were suddenly gone from the earth?

Adaptations

Adaptations can sometimes happen very quickly, over a relatively short number of generations. For example, in response to an **invasive species** of brown lizards, native green lizards in Florida began giving up their usual spots on lower tree branches and moving higher up in the trees. Because the limbs were smaller and more slippery, green lizards' toepads began growing bigger and their scales got stickier. This adaptation happened in just 15 years! That's about 20 generations, and it may seem like a long time to you, but scientists find it absolutely incredible.

Activity

POND EXPLORATION KIT

Explore life in the water with this pond exploration kit. Using a dip net, scoop up tiny critters and pond life to examine them close up, and use the underwater viewer to get a clear look at the habitat and residents themselves.

Caution: Never go near water without an adult.

❱ **Remove the lid from a coffee can.** Use the can opener to cut the bottom of the can off completely so you have a metal cylinder.

❱ **Stretch plastic wrap as tightly as you can across the top of the can** and wrap the rubber bands securely around the can to keep the plastic wrap tight. Make sure the plastic wrap has no holes so water won't seep in!

❱ **Wade out slowly into a pond** or kneel beside the water. Push your viewer down into the water as deep as you can without it filling with water. What do you spot beneath the surface?

❱ **To make a dip net, attach the handle of a kitchen strainer to a broom handle using duct tape.** Tape it very tightly so it doesn't fall off. Fill a shallow container with some pond water for a catch basin.

❱ **Use your dip net to reach into the pond and gently scoop through the water.** Try doing one sweep from the top of the pond, examine it, then do a sweep from the middle of the pond, and finally one from the bottom of the pond.

❱ **Let the water drain through the strainer,** then gently tap the contents into the catch basin. Examine the critters you've found.

Think About It

Can you spot any adaptations on the organisms you observe in the pond? Why might these adaptations have evolved? Draw diagrams of them in your science journal.

Activity

MAKE YOUR OWN BIODIVERSITY JOURNAL

❯ **Pick three very different areas to explore.** You might choose your backyard, a hike in a local forest, or your next vacation to the beach.

❯ **Grab your science journal** and something to write with.

❯ **Plan on spending at least an hour strolling slowly through each chosen environment.** Carefully observe everything you possibly can, writing down everything about it. For instance, examine the living things you see—use care and stay safe, though. Don't touch any living thing!

* What kinds of bugs are in the soil or sand?
* What about the soil itself—is it damp, dry, mossy with plant life?
* What about the trees—how is their bark different?
* Do you see any creatures—birds or small mammals, for instance?

❯ **Record all the notes you can,** and take photos or make drawings if you'd like, too. When you're finished, compare your three environments. How have each of the living organisms adapted to be perfectly suited to those environments?

Think About It

What would happen if one of the creatures or plants from one environment were suddenly brought to another environment? How would they fare? How might they adapt? And how might they impact the native plants and animals that already live in that environment?

POLLUTION

As you've seen, the environment is made up of systems, cycles, and specialized relationships between living and non-living things. When everything's working the way it should, all the living organisms within the environment—including people—are healthy and thriving.

But when something harmful is introduced to the cycle, or part of the cycle is disrupted somehow, it can cause a chain reaction of problems right through the rest of the system. These changes can hurt the health and well-being of living organisms.

One of these negative changes is pollution, which is the result of unnatural elements entering the environment. Unfortunately, humans are usually at fault. Anything that's harmful to the environment is pollution—litter, car exhaust, motor oil, used tires, smoke, chemicals. All of this can have an impact on the health of our Earth.

ESSENTIAL QUESTION

Do you think it's possible for humans to live on Earth and not produce a single bit of pollution?

Pollution

For example, **herbicides** are meant to kill unwanted plants or weeds. **Pesticides** are used to kill insects. Both can enter the soil, water, and air, contaminating them and causing harm to all living organisms.

Pollution is like the food in an unhealthy diet. If you eat a lot of junk, your body simply can't function the way it should. It's the same with the systems on our planet.

Even though **pollutants** have done a lot of damage to the environment, that doesn't mean it's "game over" for Earth. We can tackle the problem in two ways. First, clean up what we can. And second, act to prevent further pollution.

> **WORDS TO KNOW**
>
> **herbicide:** a chemical used to kill unwanted plants such as weeds.
>
> **pesticide:** a chemical used to kill pests such as rodents or insects.
>
> **pollutant:** a substance that pollutes, or dirties, the planet.

> **DID YOU KNOW?**
>
> The most common garbage along highways comes from fast food wrappers.

LAND POLLUTION

Much of the pollution on land comes from litter. People toss away garbage instead of disposing of it properly. The trash clogs up the land and attracts pests such as insects and rodents. It can harm the soil and the critters that live there if the garbage contains chemicals.

Pollution on the coast of Guyana
credit: Nils Ally CC BY 3.0

PLANET EARTH

WORDS TO KNOW

biodegrade: to decay or break down naturally.

marine: of or relating to the ocean.

landfill: a huge area of land where trash gets buried.

hazardous waste: a waste with properties that make it dangerous or capable of having a harmful effect on human health or the environment.

Most man-made objects take an extremely long time to break down, so they just lay where they've been left for years and years. If a material is made of an organic substance, it will **biodegrade**, but that process can still take a long time. And if garbage kills the plants in an area by covering them up, this affects the food chain, since green plants are the start of each chain. The garbage also affects the air quality, since plants help clean the air.

In just the United States alone, smokers consume more than 300 billion cigarettes every year—and many smokers just flick their cigarette butts on the ground instead of disposing of them properly. Cigarette butts are the most common type of litter in the United States! While the tobacco and paper parts of a cigarette break down, the plastic filters inside don't. They stick around in the environment for years. When **marine** and land animals mistake them for food and try to eat them—they die.

Plastic is especially tough on the environment, because it takes so long to break down. In fact, our oceans and beaches have become filled with plastic trash. For example, plastic straws have been one of the most common items found during beach cleanup days.

DID YOU KNOW? The chemicals in cigarettes kill the Daphnia, a microscopic aquatic animal that is important in the marine food chain.

Plastics are used for many products

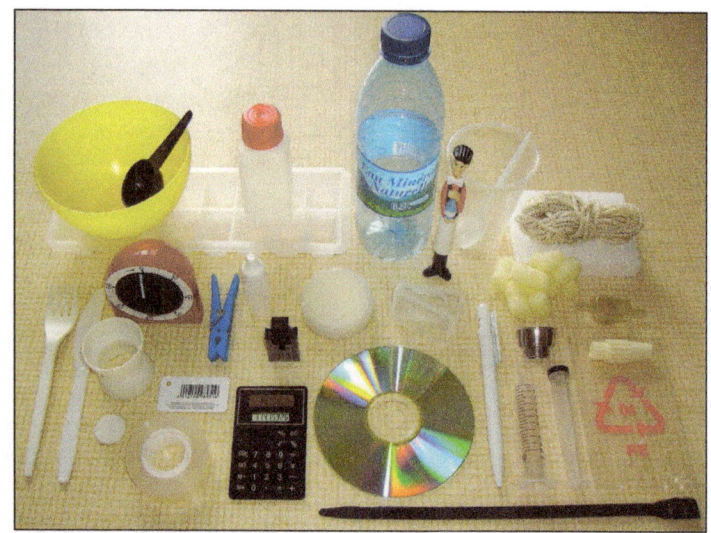

58

Pollution

In 2018, many cities and countries, and even corporations such as Starbucks, began campaigning to eliminate plastic straws altogether!

Plastic grocery bags are a particularly large problem for our planet. That's because there are so many of them—think about how many people you see, every day, carrying products out of a store in plastic bags! And what happens to those bags? How often do you see people returning the bags to the recycling bins at the store (if your store even has one)? In some areas, plastic bags are not only being discouraged—they're actively banned!

You might not think crumpling up a gum wrapper and tossing it on the ground is really that big a deal. But consider this. More than 7 billion people live in the world. If everyone dropped one crumpled gum wrapper, the wrappers would go around the whole earth about seven times! And people are tossing a lot more than just gum wrappers on the ground.

Even the trash we dispose of properly can be a problem. Where does all the garbage go? **Landfills** are areas where communities dump their solid waste. Some landfills accept **hazardous waste** and some are "sanitary" landfills with protective barriers. Other landfills are "dumps," with no protection for the environment or the living things nearby.

Welcome to the landfill

PLANET EARTH

> **WORDS TO KNOW**
>
> **acid rain:** precipitation that has been polluted by acid.
>
> **combustion engine:** an engine that burns fuel to produce energy.

AIR POLLUTION

Some pollutants that enter the air come from natural sources. When a volcano erupts, for example, volcanic ash blasts into the air, where it can remain for years. The larger the volcanic eruption, the bigger the cloud of ash and droplets of **acid rain** that enter the atmosphere.

If the cloud is large enough, it can actually spread around the entire world and affect global temperatures. Other natural sources of air pollution include smoke from forest fires and dust and sand from storms.

Keeping the Land Clean

Here are some things you can do to battle pollution.

› Keep a garbage bag in your car to collect any food wrappers or other trash you accumulate while you're traveling.

› Pick up and dispose of any trash you see, whether you're hiking, riding your bike around the neighborhood, or vacationing at the beach. Don't forget to wear thick gloves for safety!

› Minimize the amount of garbage your family generates by using re-useable containers, buying only what you really need, and giving away or donating items you don't need any more rather than tossing them out.

› Encourage your school, local parks, or other places in your community to provide trash cans in convenient locations to make it easier for everyone to toss their junk appropriately.

› Try to use natural methods, rather than chemicals, to eliminate insects and unwanted weeds.

Pollution

Airborne pollutants make it tough to breathe and can even cause diseases, such as cancer. And because winds crisscross the globe, they pick up pollutants and carry them all over the world. This is how areas far from where the actual pollution is created can become affected, too. Air pollution is not just a local concern.

While some sources of air pollution are natural, most air pollutants come from things we do ourselves—or things people have invented, such as the **combustion engine**, which uses fossil fuels.

DID YOU KNOW? In April 1815, Tambora Volcano in Indonesia erupted. It was the most powerful eruption in recorded history. Global temperatures went down as much as 3 degrees Celsius for so long that 1816 was called "the year without a summer."

All living organisms are made up of the element carbon. Plants and animals that died hundreds of millions of years ago were gradually buried and exposed to heat and pressure for all that time. The heat and pressure fossilized these dead plants and animals into what we call fossil fuels—coal, oil, and natural gas. Burning these fossil fuels produces carbon dioxide, which contributes to the pollution in our atmosphere.

Air pollution caused by factories

PLANET EARTH

> **WORDS TO KNOW**
>
> **crude oil:** petroleum oil as it comes out of the earth, before it is refined into other products.
>
> **respiratory:** having to do with breathing.
>
> **clear-cut logging:** a process in which all or almost all the trees in an area are chopped down.
>
> **emissions:** something that is sent or given out, such as smoke, gas, heat, or light.
>
> **smog:** fog combined with smoke or other pollutants.

Some elements of air pollution from burning fossil fuels include the following.

- Sulfur dioxide, formed when coal and **crude oil** are burned. It enters the air and contributes to **respiratory** illnesses such as asthma, particularly in children and the elderly. It can also affect people with heart and lung disease.

- Mono-nitrogen oxide, produced by combustion engines, causing smog.

- Carbon monoxide, another toxic product of combustion engines.

- Particulate matter, such as smoke and dust, which can come from many sources, including factory smokestacks and **clear-cut logging**.

The problem is that humans have become very dependent on fossil fuels. Not only do they hurt the environment when we use them, but they're also limited in quantity. There is only so much of them to dig up out of the earth.

Acting Globally

The Paris Agreement is an attempt on the part of world leaders to align climate goals and reduce carbon **emissions** to keep the global average temperature from rising more than 2 degrees Celsius above pre-industrial levels, starting in the year 2020. As of November 2018, 195 members of the United Nations Framework Convention on Climate Change have signed the agreement. While the United States had originally signed the agreement, in 2017, President Donald Trump announced his intention to withdraw the United States from the agreement. As different parties come into power, policies can change according to that administration's priorities. This shows just how complicated solving global climate change can be!

Keeping the Air Clean

You can reduce air pollution by taking these actions.

› Turn off electronics and lights when you're not using them. This is easy, and it really helps in the long run. Your home could be burning more fossil fuels than driving a car all around town!

› Scientists hope LED (light emitting diode) lights will reduce the amount of carbon in the environment, and they're recommended by energy specialists. They last longer, they consume lower amounts of power, and they do not contain mercury in the bulb.

› Ask your parents to turn off their engines in the carpool lane if they're waiting a long time. Have your school pass out reminders to parents.

› Help your parents plan errands so you can get everything done in one trip instead of going out several times.

› Ask your parents to use less air conditioning in the summer or turn down the heat in the winter. Wear slippers or a sweater when it's chilly.

We use fossil fuels for more than just driving our cars. We use oil and gas to heat our homes and coal powers some electrical plants. But burning all that fossil fuel is choking our atmosphere. Even as people turn to alternative energy sources such as solar and wind, many industries still rely on fossil fuels.

The ozone that's close to the ground is primarily formed by human activities such as burning fossil fuels.

Watch this amazing video showing smog rolling into Beijing.

euronews smog Beijing

Remember, ozone that is up high in the stratosphere is helpful—it shields us from harmful ultraviolet rays—but ozone closer to Earth is bad. When you see it in the form of smog, it can be harmful to your health. The amount of ozone can be so bad on hot days that health warnings advise people to stay indoors and avoid breathing in the polluted air.

PLANET EARTH

WORDS TO KNOW

sewage: waste from buildings, carried away through sewers.

sediment: material deposited by water, wind, or glaciers.

runoff: produced when water picks up wastes as it flows over the surface of the ground. Runoff can pollute streams, lakes, rivers, and oceans.

WATER POLLUTION

When **sewage**, oil, chemicals, and other pollutants enter the water cycle, the result can be devastating and even deadly. **Sediments** that collect in the water from trash or chemicals in the water prevent fish from filtering oxygen through their gills, and the fish can suffocate. When the dissolved oxygen in water drops below a certain level (two to five parts per million gallons of water), many types of fish and aquatic animals can't survive.

Aquatic plants also are "choked" and die, disrupting entire food chains.

Beach pollution from garbage washed ashore
credit: Loranchat (CC BY 3.0)

Pollution

Pollutants can come from different sources, including these.

- Sewage and farm waste can introduce harmful bacteria.

- Herbicides, pesticides, and fertilizers from agriculture can wash into the water.

- Industries sometimes dump their wastewater, which often contains acids, oils, harmful bacteria, and poisons.

- Beachgoers and boaters often leave their trash behind.

- Silt from construction or land-clearing sites can enter rivers, ponds, and other waterways through **runoff**.

Natural Repellents

Nature handles pests without all the chemicals—and we could learn a thing or two if we paid attention! Here are some natural ways to try repelling pests.

Ladybug feeding on aphids

› Ladybugs are natural predators of aphids—encourage them to live in your garden.

› Fill a zipper bag with water and hang it near entryways to discourage houseflies. Some people believe flies are scared away when they see their magnified reflection in the water. Science has yet to prove that this method works—maybe you can experiment with it!

› Use herbal oils to repel mosquitoes, fleas, and ticks.

› Got fleas? Set a shallow bowl filled with soapy water on the floor and direct the light from a desk lamp onto it in a dark room. The fleas will hop to the light and get caught in the soapy water.

PLANET EARTH

WORDS TO KNOW

bird of prey: a bird that is a predator and eats other animals.

preen: when birds groom their feathers with their beaks.

You probably remember that the water cycle includes the ocean, so pollutants that enter the water cycle can end up harming marine life and disrupting the marine food chain. What's more, the effect of harmful pollutants can be felt all the way up the food chain.

Suppose tiny copepods, which are small marine critters that look like a teardrop, absorb a pollutant into their bodies. A small fish consumes many copepods, making the concentration of pollutant greater in the body of that fish. Then, a larger fish eats lots of small fish, and that one has a higher concentration in its body, and on up the food chain.

In fact, this is how an insecticide called DDT caused a decline in **birds of prey** in the United States. The birds were eating fish with high levels of the insecticide, and it made the shells of the bird eggs very weak and thin. The eggs couldn't hatch, and the population of the birds dropped. Since the insecticide was banned, though, birds of prey have made a fantastic comeback.

DID YOU KNOW?
Only about 1 percent of all the water in the world is available for us to drink. The rest is too salty or frozen. That's why it's so important to keep it clean!

Keeping the Water Clean

Try these actions to help stop water pollution.

› Keep oil and grease out of storm drains.

› Use flea combs on your pets instead of pesticides.

› Be sure to pick up after beach visits.

› Tackle weeds the old-fashioned way—yank 'em out.

› Carpool to school, take the bus, ride your bike, or walk.

See if your local waterways have been checked for pollution at this website.

EPA my waterway

ACID RAIN

When pollutants such as sulfur dioxide and nitrogen oxides enter the air, they join water droplets and form acid rain. Anything that acid rain falls on is affected in some way. The soil can become acidic and the water chemistry can change. Acid rain can even wear away statues and rock! Historical monuments, old gravestones, and other building structures are permanently damaged by acid rain.

Acid rain damaged this gargoyle statue.
credit: Nino Barbieri (CC BY 2.5)

Acid rain can be deadly for some aquatic organisms and some soil-living creatures, such as the ones you might have spotted with the Berlese-Tullgren funnel. And that means—you guessed it—the food web is disrupted at the

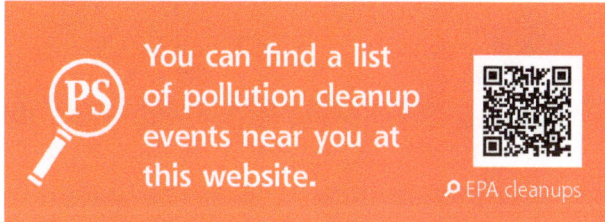

You can find a list of pollution cleanup events near you at this website.

EPA cleanups

very beginning. Plants wither and die from the acid in the water and soil, and the acid can even weaken trees and make them vulnerable to diseases.

OIL SPILLS

When a massive amount of dense, thick, natural crude oil is released into water by accident, the marine life suffers greatly. Marine mammals and birds become coated in the oil and can't easily clean it off. Birds can't maintain their body temperature or fly when their feathers are coated in oil. When they **preen**, they swallow the oil and die.

PLANET EARTH

Oil spills are difficult to clean up because water currents carry oil over large distances. Scooping up oil from the water or cleaning it off rocks or sandy beaches is an incredibly tough job.

You can see for yourself how oil spreads over water. Try tossing a handful of stale, unbuttered, unsalted popcorn into a natural body of water. Watch how quickly the kernels

Trying to clean up an oil spill
credit: NOAA Response Restoration

drift away from each other and around the water. You can imagine how a large pool of oil, floating on the surface of the water, can easily spread over a large area of ocean, riding the currents.

What does all of this pollution mean for Planet Earth? Why should we care so much if things are a little dirty? Well, that pollution has some major repercussions—climate change. The character of our planet is changing a rapid rate, faster than most living things can adapt. We'll take a closer look at climate change in the next chapter.

> **ESSENTIAL QUESTION**
>
> Do you think it's possible for humans to live on Earth and not produce a single bit of pollution?

Oily Feathers

If you find a feather, look at it closely. You can see little "hooks" where the individual pieces of the feather cling together along the shaft. If you pull gently, you can separate them, but if you smooth it carefully, they'll cling back together. Now try putting a drop or two of vegetable oil on the feather. When you separate the feather this time, it won't go back together properly. That's what birds face when they're covered in oil from a spill.

Activity

MAKE YOUR OWN EFFECTS OF ACIDS EXPERIMENT

You can see for yourself the impact that acid has on the environment.

❱ **Gather various elements you find in nature**—such as eggshell pieces, seashells, different types of rocks, clean chicken bones, green leaves, etc.

❱ **Place each object in a separate, small container.** Using an acid such as vinegar, submerge each object.

❱ **Check back on your project at regular intervals and record your findings.**

✱ What happens to each of the objects?

✱ Do some last longer than others?

✱ Do some seem to remain untouched?

Try This!

Drop a piece of chalk into a glass, then pour vinegar, which is acidic, to cover it. What happens to the chalk? The result is similar to what acid rain does to rocks and statues over time.

Think About It

What objects were impacted the most—and how do you think their reaction would change the balance of the environment and life in it? What are some ways we can protect the environment from this kind of damage? For the objects that seem unchanged, do you think if you left them longer, they would eventually show signs of impact? Why or why not?

Activity

AIR POLLUTION COLLECTION CARDS

Want to see what you are breathing? Air pollution is a major problem in many regions. Particles that don't belong in our lungs end up there because they are in the air we breathe! Use your own air collection cards to see just how much dirt you're sucking down.

> **Collect five index cards and label them,** "Kitchen," "Laundry Room," "Bedroom," "Front Yard," and "Backyard."

> **Smear the front of every card with Vaseline.** Make sure the whole card is coated!

> **Tape these cards in the appropriate places.** Every day for five days, check your cards. Take a photo or draw the card in your science journal so you can see how much pollution has collected on the card.

DID YOU KNOW?

Noise pollution is a very real threat to wildlife—very loud noises from machinery or vehicles can disrupt animals' **migration** and breeding and limit their choice of habitat.

Think About It

At the end of five days, determine which area has the most air pollution. Why do you think this is the case? Are there things you can do to reduce the amount of pollution released into the air in that space?

WORDS TO KNOW

migration: moving from one place to another, often with the change in seasons.

CLIMATE CHANGE

Chapter 6

If you've ever stepped into a greenhouse, you can understand what the buzz is all about when people talk about climate change and the **greenhouse effect**. The glass of a greenhouse allows the sun's rays inside, but doesn't allow them to exit as easily. The result? The temperature inside the greenhouse rises and the air there is hotter than the air outside.

ESSENTIAL QUESTION

Why is it difficult for some people to believe that climate change is a concern?

In a nutshell, that's what global warming is all about. Of course, no glass ceiling covers the earth—it's a bit more complicated than that. After all, in many places, it still feels pretty cold in the winter. Plus, much of the polar regions are still covered in ice, right?

71

PLANET EARTH

WORDS TO KNOW

greenhouse effect: when the presence in the atmosphere of gases such as carbon dioxide, water vapor, and methane allow incoming sunlight to pass through, but absorb heat radiated back from the earth's surface, trapping solar radiation.

drought: a long period of little or no rain.

magnify: to enlarge.

greenhouse gas: a gas that traps heat in the earth's atmosphere and contributes to the greenhouse effect and global warming.

When you think about climate change, however, you need to think of the entire planet, not just one region. Climate is the pattern of weather during a long period of time—decades instead of seasons. Scientists measure the global climate by finding the average of temperatures across all regions of the earth, during all the seasons. And evidence shows, the planet is warming up

Scientists have found that the global temperature has increased more than 1 degree Fahrenheit since 1880, when scientists began keeping track. Doesn't sound like a lot, does it? But even one degree of difference can start glaciers melting and animals migrating to adapt to changes brought about in their environment because of the temperature changes.

In extremely bad droughts, crops can fail.

Just one degree of temperature change can change weather patterns and ecosystems.

It can lead to extreme **drought** in some areas and extremes in high rainfall in others. Have you ever experienced a drought? Have you been hit with an extreme weather event, such as a hurricane?

Many areas have seen an increase in hurricanes because of warmer water temperatures and hot, dry summers riddled with periods of drought. Increased flooding is another major problem as rainstorms grow more severe. What's more, if the trend continues as scientists predict, that one-degree rise will turn into two degrees, then three, and the problems associated with climate change will **magnify** and increase in frequency.

GREENHOUSE GASES

Under normal conditions, sunlight radiates down to Earth and warms the land and the water, creating ideal conditions for life. Some of the energy is reflected back into the atmosphere, where gases called **greenhouse gases** trap part of that energy to maintain a comfortable living temperature on the planet. We need some greenhouse gases for life to flourish here.

In a healthy atmosphere, the rest of the energy is radiated back out into space. But when the greenhouse gases get too thick, very little heat can radiate back into the atmosphere, and our planet's thermostat starts to rise past a healthy level. And that's where global warming starts.

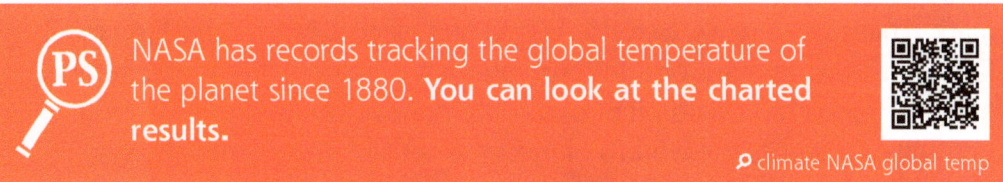

NASA has records tracking the global temperature of the planet since 1880. **You can look at the charted results.**

🔍 climate NASA global temp

PLANET EARTH

> **WORDS TO KNOW**
>
> **flora:** the plant life in an ecosystem.

The earth has naturally occurring greenhouse gases, including water vapor, that have protected the planet throughout its life. And greenhouse gases such as carbon dioxide, methane, and nitrous oxide are all naturally occurring in the atmosphere, too. However, human activity has added more of these gases into the environment than it can handle, making the atmosphere too clogged up for some of the radiation to escape back into space. The buildup of gases contributes to the greenhouse effect of rising temperatures.

Carbon dioxide, the biggest pollutant, is primarily formed when we burn fossil fuels for energy, such as when we drive gas-powered cars.

Carbon dioxide makes up the largest percentage of greenhouse gases. Some carbon dioxide, however, comes from natural sources—for example, when animals, including humans, breathe or when living things die and decay. But the majority of carbon dioxide in the atmosphere comes from other human activities.

About one third of the carbon dioxide in the atmosphere comes from our sources of transportation—cars, buses, trucks, airplanes. A little less than one-fourth of the carbon dioxide comes from lighting and heating our homes. The rest comes from factories and businesses.

It's Electric!

By 2017, the sales of electric and plug-in hybrid cars topped the 3 million mark. That's good news, because hybrid and electric cars cut back on fossil fuel use as well as emissions. Industry analysts predict that the total number of battery-powered cars on the road could rise to close to 5 million soon. Currently, China has the world's biggest market for electric cars.

Climate Change

Trees and plants take carbon dioxide from the air to use in photosynthesis. In a natural balance, everything would work out perfectly—animals would breathe in oxygen and breathe out carbon dioxide, and plants would take in carbon dioxide and return oxygen to the atmosphere. But when the balance is disturbed and the atmosphere has far too much carbon dioxide, our planet's **flora** can't absorb it fast enough to maintain a balance.

That spells trouble for the atmosphere—and in return, trouble right here on Earth. That's why it's so important to keep our existing trees healthy and to plant new ones. And to try to limit the activities that emit carbon dioxide.

Methane is the next most common greenhouse gas. Cattle are a big natural source of methane as they break down their food and "break wind!" With about 1.5 billion cows in the world, that's a lot of methane!

However, the biggest source of methane comes from landfills, where waste breaks down and releases the gas. It's also released during coal mining and the making of petroleum-based products.

The greener the earth, the healthier it will be

PLANET EARTH

> **WORDS TO KNOW**
>
> **chlorofluorocarbons (CFCs):** simple gases that contain carbon, chlorine, fluorine, and sometimes hydrogen, that are a major cause of stratospheric ozone depletion.
>
> **carbon footprint:** the total amount of carbon dioxide and other greenhouse gases emitted over the full life cycle of a product or service, or by a person or family in a year.
>
> **hydroelectricity:** electricity created by the flow of water.

Nitrous oxide is another greenhouse gas. It's produced naturally by bacteria in the soil. The human contribution to nitrous oxide comes from the use of nitrogen-based fertilizers. Although nitrous oxide isn't present in quantities as large as carbon dioxide or methane, the chemical makeup of nitrous oxide causes it to trap more energy in the atmosphere than carbon dioxide—almost 300 times more!

Aerosol cans, such as those used to hold whipped cream and cooking spray, need a propellant to squirt out their contents. Years ago, the propellants used were **chlorofluorocarbons (CFCs)**. These chemicals were found to weaken the ozone in the stratosphere. CFCs are now banned in spray cans and foam packaging, so aerosols use different propellants to spray. One of those is sometimes nitrous oxide.

DID YOU KNOW? One little critter—the termite—is responsible for a whopping 11 percent of global methane emissions from natural sources.

WHAT CAN YOU DO?

Sometimes, it's easy to think you aren't making an impact on the world if you plant a tree or recycle a soda can. After all, you're just one person. It's just one tree. But think about what nature shows us—a nest of ants, together, can tackle a much larger invader and win! It's because they're working together. So, consider getting a group of friends or neighbors together.

You can organize lots of community projects to help the environment.

What's Your Carbon Footprint?

How much of an impact you have on the environment—that is, how much your activities add carbon dioxide to the atmosphere—is measured and represented in what's called a **carbon footprint**. The larger your number, the greater your impact, like a giant footprint upon the earth. Ideally, when people see in plain numbers how much their lifestyles are affecting the planet, they take steps to make changes and reduce that carbon footprint. They start making choices that are gentler on the earth.

Calculate your family's carbon footprint at this website.

carbon footprint calculator

The calculation of a carbon footprint is based on different factors. Here's what is measured and why.

› **Where you live.** Your location often determines how your home is powered. Depending on where you live, your home could receive electricity from coal, **hydroelectricity**, or natural gas.

› **How much electricity your household uses.** Calculates the amount of power used.

› **How many people are in your family.** More people in one home use more appliances and energy.

› **What kind of car your family drives and how far.** Does your family have a fuel-efficient car? Do you drive long distances to go to school or the store? This has an effect on your carbon footprint.

› **Airplane trips you take.** Airplanes use a lot of fuel, especially on takeoff. The more trips you take, the more fuel is being consumed to get you there.

PLANET EARTH

> **WORDS TO KNOW**
>
> **ozone depletion:** the thinning of the ozone layer.

Here are some ideas for environmental projects.

Restore wildlife habitat. Pick up the trash and replant native plants to encourage wildlife in neglected or unused areas.

Use school grounds. Talk to a teacher about a school-wide project. Build a pond to host local wildlife or a community garden to encourage people to cut down on produce they buy from faraway places. Food that is grown elsewhere must be shipped to your area, which uses fuel.

Take on the carpool. Do you ever see people sitting in their cars with the engine idling? Many schools and businesses don't allow idling on the grounds anymore, but people still run their cars as they wait. Do some research and create a pamphlet that shows the effects of releasing carbon dioxide into the atmosphere. Educate people so they can make healthier choices!

Working together in a community garden
credit: U.S. Air Force photo by Linda LaBonte Britt

Create an errand pool. Coordinate an errand pool with neighbors to reduce the amount of driving everyone does. Families can take turns running errands or pick things up for one another to reduce special trips to the store.

DID YOU KNOW? Poison ivy likes carbon dioxide. The more carbon dioxide in the environment, the bigger poison ivy grows.

OZONE DEPLETION

Another environmental problem that gets a lot of headlines is **ozone depletion**. Remember, ozone is a gas that's made of molecules formed by three oxygen atoms. The oxygen we breathe is made of two oxygen atoms.

When it's close to the ground, ozone is toxic and unwanted, but in the stratosphere, ozone in needed to protect the earth from the sun's UV rays.

Up in the stratosphere, ozone is naturally formed when the sun's UV light hits oxygen (O) in the air. The oxygen molecules split up, and the atoms rejoin as ozone (O_3) molecules. They're small but they're mighty, blocking harmful UV rays from reaching the earth.

When certain gases, such as chlorine, enter the atmosphere, they tear apart the ozone molecules. The big culprits are CFCs, chemicals made of chlorine, fluorine, and carbon.

When CFCs were invented in the 1930s, they were considered wonder chemicals. They were cheap and easy to produce, so CFCs were used in many different products, such as propellants in spray cans—think hair spray, bug spray, and deodorant. They were also used in foam food packaging and other things made from Styrofoam.

By the early 1970s, however, scientists realized that those CFCs were floating up into the atmosphere. What was happening up in the stratosphere was cause for alarm.

The sun's ultraviolet rays were breaking apart the CFCs and releasing the chlorine. That chlorine was "attacking" our protective ozone shield, allowing ultraviolet rays to reach down to Earth. One chlorine molecule can destroy up to 100,000 ozone molecules!

CFCs are tough stuff. They don't break down easily, and they hang around in the environment for more than 100 years. And CFCs take around 50 years to travel up to the stratosphere.

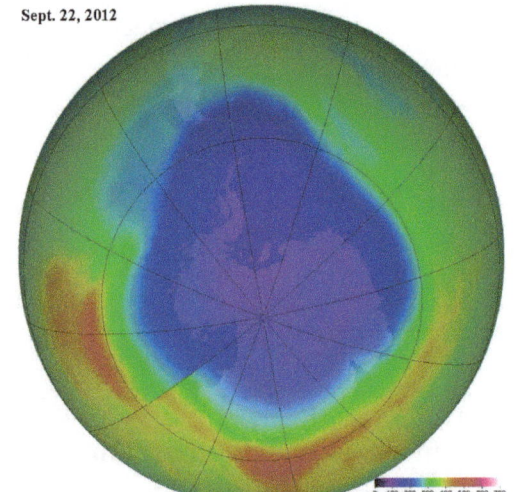

Antarctic ozone hole in 2012
credit: NASA

Fortunately, CFCs were banned in 1978 in industrialized nations. That means that today's aerosol cans don't contribute any CFCs, and foam doesn't contain any CFCs, either. But those CFCs released in 1970 won't even start attacking the ozone until around the year 2020.

Here's some good news: Scientists say the ozone hole is shrinking and has reached its smallest size since 1988! It's possible that warmer-than-usual weather conditions have helped contribute to the shrinkage, since warmer air helps minimize ozone-gobbling chemicals such as chlorine and bromine.

 See an animation of the ozone layer over the Antarctic for the past several decades. What do you notice?

ozonewatch movie

But that doesn't mean we should stop working to help our atmosphere—there's still work to be done!

ULTRAVIOLET RAYS

Why are UV rays so harmful? The sun's light comes to the earth in the form of wavelengths that are invisible to the human eye—ultraviolet rays. Two types of ultraviolet rays reach the earth's surface—UV-a and UV-b.

Both UV-a and UV-b rays are bad for human skin. UV-a rays penetrate our skin more deeply and can cause long-term skin damage, such as wrinkles. Scientists also believe that UV-a rays play a role in some skin cancers. UV-b rays cause sunburn and are thought to cause most skin cancers.

DID YOU KNOW? The word *ozone* comes from the Greek word meaning "smelly," because it has a very sharp odor.

PLANET EARTH

WORDS TO KNOW

cataract: a clouding of the eye's natural lens.

correlate: a relationship between two things that affect or impact one another.

So, if the ozone in the stratosphere can't do its job and block the UV rays, people will have a greater risk of health troubles. UV rays may also cause a gradual clouding of the lens of the eye, a condition called **cataracts**. How can you protect yourself from the sun's harmful rays? Wear a hat and sunglasses and put on lots of sunscreen!

Humans aren't the only ones hurt by too much exposure to UV rays. Some types of tiny plankton can be affected by high levels of UV rays, which either kills them or causes them to sink deeper into the ocean. Going deeper means the plant plankton won't get enough of the light they need to photosynthesize.

The "Hole" Story

The ozone layer surrounding the globe is getting thinner everywhere, but in some places it's worse than others. A significant thinning occurs seasonally over Antarctica. It's not an actual "hole," really—just super-thin ozone, but it's referred to as a hole. During spring in Antarctica—September through November—up to 60 percent of the ozone in the stratosphere is lost above the big, icy continent. Why in the spring? During the winter, Antarctica has the coldest temperatures in the world and receives no sunlight. Strong, swirling winds create clouds that release chlorine into the atmosphere. When the sun hits the chlorine in the spring, it goes to work tearing apart ozone molecules. Later, as the winds calm and the temperature rises, the ozone grows thicker again. Scientists worry that more "holes" will open up in the ozone around the world, and that one day, they may not thicken back up. Similar ozone loss takes place in the Arctic polar regions. It's called a "dimple," since it's not as severe as Antarctica's ozone loss.

DID YOU KNOW?

In September 2017, the ozone hole was about 7.6 million square miles wide—and it shrank by 1.3 million square miles since then!

Global Warming: Fact or Fiction?

Some people don't believe that global warming is the result of human actions. They think that it's a natural progression of Earth's cycles. There is evidence that the planet has cycled through many periods of natural heating and cooling. During the days of the dinosaur, the earth was warmer than it is today and few or no polar ice caps existed. But scientists point out that those cycles took place gradually. What's different today is that our recent warming has happened during a relatively short period of time that **correlates** to our heavy use of fossil fuels. Plus, no matter the underlying cause of climate change, it's still wise to take steps to care for our planet and reduce our dependency on limited fuel sources.

And, as you know, plankton are the foundation of the marine food chain. Any disruption to the plankton population means trouble for the rest of marine life—and humans, too.

Plants and crops can also be affected by harmful UV rays, although scientists are still studying the impact. Some types of plants are more affected than others—for example, one type of rice plant is negatively affected by too many UV-b rays, but another type of rice plant doesn't show any signs of trouble at all.

Climate change is a problem that will take the combined effort of all individuals, businesses, and governments to solve.

In the next chapter, we'll learn about some of the steps you can start taking immediately to improve the health of the planet.

ESSENTIAL QUESTION

Why is it difficult for some people to believe that climate change is a concern?

Activity

GLOBAL WARMING IN A JAR

Here's an easy way to see the effect of the sun's energy on air that's "trapped" versus heated air that can freely move around. Start a scientific method worksheet to organize your experiment.

❯ **Place one thermometer in each of two jars.** Leave one jar uncovered. Cover the second jar with plastic wrap and secure it with the rubber band.

❯ **Set both jars on white paper in direct sunlight.** Be sure that the sunlight is not falling directly on the front of the thermometers—turn the jars so the sun's rays hit the back of the thermometers instead. This way, you'll be sure you are getting a reading of the air inside the jars.

❯ **The uncovered jar represents the earth with the proper amount of greenhouse gases,** which allow extra heat to escape from the atmosphere. The second jar represents the earth with a layer of greenhouse gases that is too thick.

❯ **Check on the jars every 30 minutes and record the temperatures.** Keep recording as long as you can—all day if possible. Create a chart in your science journal to record your data.

❯ **Compare the readings on the thermometers to measure the difference between the two "atmospheres."** What did you find?

Think About It

What is something you love doing or using that is harming the environment by contributing to global warming. Would you be willing to give that up forever? How about for a day? A month? What is something you could do or use that would be much healthier for the environment—and are you able to make that change right now?

Activity

PROPAGATE YOUR OWN TREE

If you've got a favorite tree in your yard, you may be able to grow another one just like it by taking a cutting and planting it. You can give your new plants as gifts to encourage other people to plant more trees, too.

> **Caution:** This activity needs adult supervision.

▶ **The best time to take a cutting from a favorite tree is early in the morning in winter, when the tree is dormant.** Willow trees grow quickly and **propagate** well, whereas apple trees are a little harder. Ask a gardener for suggestions or do some research at the library.

▶ **Clean a knife or pruning shear blades in rubbing alcohol to prevent disease from harming the tree.** Cut off the end of a branch, about 4 to 6 inches long. Remove leaves from the lower third of the cutting if there are any. Dip the cut end in rooting hormone, which you can find at a gardening center. Tap off excess.

▶ **Fill a container with a mixture of half sand, half peat.** Insert the cutting about one-third of its length into your potting soil. Keep the potting soil moist by misting the plant on a regular schedule. You can cover the cutting with plastic to protect it. Place it in a well-lit area—but not in direct light.

▶ **In the spring, very carefully brush away the sand and peat to make sure your tree has grown roots.** Transplant it into a larger container with soil. You may want to wait to transplant your tree into the ground until it's older and stronger to increase its odds of survival.

Try This!

What if you gave tree cuttings or saplings to everyone you know for the next gift-giving holiday? How many trees could you alone be responsible for adding back to the earth? What if everyone did that?

WORDS TO KNOW

dormant: in a state of rest or inactivity.

propagate: to grow, to increase the amount of something.

Activity

MAKE YOUR OWN OZONE DEPLETION EXPERIMENT

Can't imagine how gases can create a hole in the ozone? Try this quick experiment to show how the more dangerous chemicals there are in the atmosphere, the more impact they have.

Caution: Ask an adult to help you boil the water.

> **Begin by chewing pieces of gum** (set one aside to chew the other or have a friend help with one piece!). Be sure to chew until the gum is nice and soft.

> **Get two empty bottles.** Have an adult help you heat water to boiling in a kettle, and use a funnel to fill one bottle about a third of the way with hot water. Fill the second bottle all the way with hot water.

> **Carefully stretch each piece of soft,** chewed gum over the opening of each bottle.

> **Observe what happens.** Does one bottle generate more "ozone holes" than the other?

DID YOU KNOW? Scientists measure the thickness of the ozone using weather balloons, high-flying aircraft, and satellites.

Think About It

Besides reducing the amount of water ("gases"), what else could be done to minimize the holes in the gum ("ozone layer")?

Chapter 7

RECYCLING

When something is used more than once or when something old is used to make something new, that's recycling. Chances are, you and your family already recycle. Maybe you take a bin of newspapers down to the curb every week along with the garbage can, or you might take your recycling over to big community bins—sometimes organizing everything by type of material: paper, plastic, glass, aluminum, and others.

In some places, you pay a deposit on a glass bottle or aluminum can and receive that money back when you return the container to the store. When you're recycling, you're taking steps toward helping the environment—but did you ever wonder how?

ESSENTIAL QUESTION

Do you think everyone on the planet could stop buying new products for an entire week? What impact would that have on our environment?

87

PLANET EARTH

WORDS TO KNOW

recycling: shredding, squashing, pulping, or melting items to use the materials to create new products.

engineer: a person who uses science, math, and creativity to design and build things.

debris: scattered pieces of waste or remains.

extrude: when something is pushed or forced.

Recycling helps reduce the amount of garbage that ends up in landfills. It also reduces the amount of new material that needs to be used to make more things. When you recycle, you're saving the materials that new goods are made from, and you're also saving the energy that would be needed to make those new materials.

Recycling helps the environment in lots of different ways. For example, recycling paper saves natural resources by reducing the number of trees that need to be cut down to make new paper. Recycling reduces global warming because less fossil fuel needs to be burned to produce recycled materials than new materials. And recycling also saves the land by keeping materials out of landfills.

You've seen why it's important to cut down on the amount of garbage going into landfills, and you know why it's important to cut down on how much we burn fossil fuels. Recycling is one of the best ways to cut back on all that garbage and reduce fossil fuel use.

In 2015, an **engineer** came up with an idea to make roads out of recycled plastic. **Take a look at this video!**

🔎 YouTube plastic into roads

Recycling is critical
credit: Cogdogblog (CC BY 2.0)

WHERE DOES IT GO?

What happens to the materials after you drop them off for recycling? They all go to a facility to be cleaned and sorted. Then, they head to processing plants, where each of the materials goes through a process that will make it available again to manufacturing plants. This is where the recycled materials are turned into new products.

Plastic. Plastic undergoes a multi-step process to become usable again. First, the plastic is cleaned well to remove any **debris**. Then, it's shredded and washed again. The shreds are melted and **extruded** through tiny holes into strands, like plastic spaghetti. The strands are cooled, then chopped into pellets and sold to manufacturing companies. Lots of things are made from recycled plastic, even clothing!

Paper. When paper is recycled, it's sorted by grade and then broken down into a pulp. The pulp is then spread over a conveyor belt and pressed with heated rollers. The result? Big rolls of paper. Colored paper is hardest to recycle because it must have the color removed. And paper can't be recycled forever—the fibers get weak over time, and new wood pulp must be added in.

Watch how paper is recycled in factories.

How It's Made Paper Recycling

Glass. One of the best recycling materials, glass can be re-used over and over. An exception is colored glass, because the color can't be removed, so clear glass is the best. When glass is recycled, it's crushed and re-melted to make new glass. To help the recycling process, remove paper labels from your glass jars before recycling them. In some regions, glass recycling is no longer done because it's often cheaper to make new glass than recycle old glass.

PLANET EARTH

> **WORDS TO KNOW**
>
> **compost:** decayed food scraps and vegetation that can be put back in the soil or to recycle food scraps and vegetation and put them back in the soil.

Metal. As with glass and plastic, metal is melted when it's being recycled. Then, it's rolled out into thin sheets to be made into new products, such as aluminum cans. It takes far less energy to recycle cans than it does to make new cans from fresh resources.

OTHER WAYS TO RECYCLE

Sometimes, you don't even realize how much stuff you toss into the trash every day. The next time you're about to toss something in the garbage, think about it: Is this something you could possibly use again, for another purpose?

Some of the projects in this book can transform used items into something new. Save small containers and use them to sort small desk or kitchen objects. Use an old, punctured hose to water your garden. Take old milk jugs, cut them, and use them as shovels at the beach. Wash glass food jars and use them to store bulk foods or all those stray pennies, or to make decorative sand art jars for your home or for gifts. Reuse as often as possible!

Compost makes rich soil
credit: normanack (CC BY 2.0)

Another way to help is by building a **compost** bin in your backyard to take on the "brown" and "green" waste from your household. Brown waste includes paper products such as newspapers, shredded cereal boxes, and cardboard. Green waste is stuff such as grass clippings, leaves, and food waste. You can compost almost all of your food waste, except for meat.

> **Through time, the materials that you compost will rot, producing a soil you can add to the garden.**

Take a good look at the purchases you want to make before you make them. Can you avoid excess packaging by buying something else? Choose something wrapped in paper rather than plastic or foam, because paper can be composted. Could you buy a product in a larger size and share it with neighbors, friends, or family? This reduces the number of smaller packages that have to be purchased to get the same amount of that product. And even consider if you really need the item at all! Can you make do with something you already have?

PLANET EARTH

Just how much garbage does your family generate? Make a chart to find out, recording the weekly weight of your trash. Record the weight of what you recycle as well. Then, talk about the results with your family. How much of that trash can you recycle? Even better, how much can you reuse? You can issue a challenge to family members to see who can generate the least amount of trash and make individual charts. See how your family can reduce its waste over time.

Look at how the choices you make affect your family's garbage output. For example, one box of microwave popcorn might have eight individual bags of popcorn—and each of those bags also has a plastic wrapper. Just counting pieces of material, that's 17 pieces of garbage to throw out!

DID YOU KNOW? In the United States, each person throws out an average of four and a half pounds of garbage every day!

If you buy popcorn kernels instead and air-pop them or even do it the "old-fashioned" way, on the stove in a pan with oil, you'll just purchase the one bag of kernels—and you'll probably get far more than eight servings out of it, too. You can find plenty of ways to cut down on packaging waste all around your kitchen. Stop buying frozen dinners and single-serving snacks!

Popcorn is easy to make on the stove—and you can flavor it any way you want!

RECYCLING IN NATURE

You know that many cycles in nature move material through different steps—such as the water cycle. Water evaporates into water vapor, rises to the atmosphere, falls back to the earth, and is used by living organisms before it's returned to the water cycle. Nature has even more examples of recycling. The organisms that live close to the ground—insects, bacteria, fungi, and earthworms—go to work breaking down everything from living remains to logs to even some garbage people have left behind. They recycle this material into something new and useful.

The simple earthworm can help us
credit: Katja Schulz (CC BY 2.0)

Insects and earthworms can eat organic material such as dead creatures and plant materials. They produce fertile soil as their waste products after they've digested that organic material.

This helps the environment, not only by getting rid of dead organisms, but also by creating renewed soil full of nutrients for new organisms to grow in.

PLANET EARTH

> **WORDS TO KNOW**
>
> **vermicomposting:** using worms in compost to break down and recycle food wastes.
>
> **precycling:** buying less and creating less waste.

Fungi such as mushrooms, mold, and yeast, and bacteria break down plant matter through a chemical process. This reduces the matter to smaller components that can also be absorbed back into the soil, replenishing the environment and providing new materials for growing organisms.

Worms are one of the best recyclers, turning food waste into composting material to rebuild the soil. In fact, many people use **vermicomposting** to reduce household waste. Using large bins that contain bedding and worms, people add food waste for the worms to eat and break down. Some people even keep these containers right under the kitchen sink for convenience! It's similar to outdoor composting. But it's not smelly and doesn't attract insects if you put the proper waste materials in and maintain it properly.

DID YOU KNOW? Today, the United States recycles almost a third of its waste—almost twice as much as in the early 1990s.

All of your recycling efforts will help the planet recover and thrive. That means the plant and animal populations that are affected by climate change—which is all of them—will have a chance to find their balance once again. We'll take a look at this process in the next chapter.

Precycling Ideas

› If you carry your own canvas shopping bags into the store, you'll walk out with fewer plastic or paper shopping bags (or none!).

› Take fabric scraps and hem them along the edges to make cloth napkins to use instead of paper products. This is actually recycling, too!

› Use kitchen rags instead of paper towels. This is both **precycling** and recycling!

› Use rechargeable batteries.

> **ESSENTIAL QUESTION**
>
> Do you think everyone on the planet could stop buying new products for an entire week? What impact would that have on our environment?

Activity

MAKE YOUR OWN NATURALLY DYED SHOPPING TOTE

Ask your local grocer if they have any produce that needs to be thrown away. You can use dye made from this produce to decorate a shopping tote. Just don't eat any of the old produce, even if it looks like it's okay!

> **Caution:** Have an adult help you with the stove.

❯ **Crush or tear plant material** such as grass cuttings, beets, the papery outer skin of onion peels, blueberries, or other materials into small pieces. Put the pieces in a pot (one for each color) and add enough water to just cover them. If you are using onion skins, press down on them until they're compacted at the bottom of the pot.

❯ **If you're using a slow cooker, turn it on low and let the plants sit overnight or for several hours.** If you're using regular pots, put the heat on low for several hours. Don't let them simmer, or the water will evaporate.

❯ **Let the liquid cool,** then strain out the plant material over a bowl or other container. You'll be left with a natural, concentrated color dye.

❯ **Use the dyes to create a tie-dye pattern on a canvas tote.** Dip stamps into the dyes and decorate your bag or use a paintbrush. Let the tote dry completely. Use leftover dye to decorate an old T-shirt or create a fun towel for the beach.

Think About It

What other natural materials could be used to dye fabrics? Are some fabrics better suited to natural dyes than others? Why? Watch the Brooklyn Textile Arts Center dye with natural products.

🔎 The Chemistry of Natural Dyes

Activity

DO SOME VERMICOMPOSTING

Red wiggler worms can eat your leftover garbage, turning it into rich soil to use in the garden. Be sure to keep your worm box in a place that's warm and dark.

> **Caution:** Have an adult help with cutting the plastic bottle.

▶ **Cut a few inches off the top of a 2-liter bottle and put the top aside for later.** Tear or cut several pages of newspaper into strips about an inch wide. This is bedding material for your worms, and they'll break this down, too. Put some into the bottom of the bottle and lightly spritz it with water. You want it damp, but not soaking wet, or the worms will drown. Fill your bottle about half full with these fluffed up, damp newspaper strips.

▶ **Add a cup of soil and toss that with the newspaper.** Put your worms into their container, and when they've moved down away from the light, add some kitchen scraps and place a shallow layer of newspaper bedding material on top.

▶ **Poke several good-sized holes in the top of the bottle,** and tape it on top, either in an upright position or upside-down, whichever is more convenient for you. You need to be sure that enough air circulates inside your bottle.

DID YOU KNOW? The red wiggler worm is most often employed in composting bins. It's different from your average earthworm—it loves rotting vegetation and compost but doesn't do too well in "regular" soil. Your average earthworm, on the other hand, loves plain old soil!

Activity

❯ **You'll want to keep your vermicomposter out of the light.** Lay black construction paper out on a table. Cut out a few window flaps so you can see inside—but cut around only three sides of the windows. This way you can close the flaps when you're not observing your worms. When you're finished creating windows, wrap the construction paper around the bottle tightly and tape it securely.

❯ **Check regularly to make sure that the bedding stays just barely moist.** The worms will work on the food scraps and turn them into compost. Add new scraps as they break down.

❯ **If you're going to maintain your vermicomposter for a long time, you'll need to remove the compost after a while.** You can lure the worms to one side of your container by putting their food on one side, waiting a day or so for them to move over, then scooping up the compost. Replace the compost with fresh bedding. Also, keep an eye on the moisture in the bin. If it's getting too wet, poke a couple of small holes (too small for your worms to crawl out of!) in the bottom of the bin and set it in a saucer or container to catch any drips.

Red wigglers enjoy these foods.

- coffee grounds
- fruit
- vegetables
- egg shells
- used tea bags

Red wigglers don't enjoy these foods.

- meat and fish
- dairy products
- bread
- banana peels and oranges
- non-foods such as plastic

Think About It

What other natural ways are there to facilitate organic composting? How do you see composting happen in nature, on its own? Would it be possible for humans to do something similar?

Activity

MAKE YOUR OWN SCRATCH-AND-SNIFF RECYCLED PAPER

It's fun to make recycled paper, but it's even more fun to make scented paper! You can use this as writing paper or to give as a gift.

Caution: Don't pour shredded paper and water down the drain.

▶ **Shred newspaper into small pieces and put about one cup of the shreds into a blender.** Add about ¾ cup of water, then keep alternating layers of shredded paper and water until the blender is about half full. Turn the blender on at low speed until everything is all mashed together and looks like pulp. Add more water if the blender gets bogged down.

▶ **Add your scent.** Use about four drops of liquid extract such as vanilla or 2 tablespoons of powdered spice such as cinnamon. Blend again for a couple of seconds to mix it all together.

▶ **Take your mix outside.** On a flat surface, spread out a large towel or rag. Lay a fine screen on top, such as a window screen, then pour out your paper pulp onto the screen. Spread it evenly over the screen with your fingers, leaving a border of a couple of inches of screen all the way around the edges.

▶ **Lay a second screen on top so the pulp lays between the two screens and press evenly around the entire surface to push water out of the pulp.** If your towel gets saturated, carefully lift off your screen-and-paper "sandwich" and use a new towel to absorb the water. When most of the water is squeezed out, lay the whole thing out on another towel in a warm place to dry overnight. When it's dry, you can cut your paper into whatever pieces you want.

Think About It

What other ways could you make your own recycled paper fun, to encourage other people to think about recycling?

Chapter 8

FINDING THE
BALANCE

Human activity causes the most problems in the environment. As the human population grows, we draw upon the land and its resources more and more for food, water, energy, and space to live on. Our **ancestors** didn't realize just how delicate the environment is, so they, too, made mistakes and caused damage to the environment.

ESSENTIAL QUESTION

Think of one extinct species. How would life today be different if that species were still around?

Some of this damage includes **overhunting** animals and releasing harmful chemicals into the environment. Through actions such as these, humans have been the cause or part of the cause of the **extinction** of many different species.

PLANET EARTH

WORDS TO KNOW

ancestors: the people who lived before you.

overhunting: when an animal is hunted in great numbers, so much that their population falls to low levels. This can cause extinction.

extinction: when a species dies out and there are no more left in the world.

endangered: a species of plant or animal with a very low population that is at risk of disappearing entirely.

nocturnal: describes an animal that is active at night instead of during the day.

crops: plants grown for food and other uses.

WHAT CAUSES EXTINCTION?

Different roads lead to extinction. An animal or plant might be exposed to any one of these, or, more likely, several.

Excessive hunting. The great auk was a large, penguin-type bird that lived along North Atlantic coastlines. It was hunted in great numbers, and even its eggs were prized and removed from the wild. The bird couldn't reproduce faster than it was being killed. In the mid 1800s, the last great auk died and the species became extinct.

Non-native species. Every biome has its unique balance between climate, geology, and living organisms. When that balance is disrupted, it can mean the end for some species. That's what happened to the birds on the island of Guam.

DID YOU KNOW?
Almost 2,000 plant and animal species around the world are threatened or **endangered**.

In the late 1940s, the tree snake arrived on the island, most likely as a stowaway on a ship. The birds in Guam had never had to deal with snakes as predators, so they had no natural defenses against these tree-dwelling serpents. The result? The **nocturnal** snakes had an easy time catching the birds. After about 40 years, very few birds remained on the island and several species became extinct.

A drawing of the extinct great auk

100

Finding the Balance

Destruction of habitat. In the 1930s, the last heath hen died. Its extinction was blamed partially on overhunting and disease. A big reason for the heath hen's extinction, however, was the conversion of the its natural habitat along the East Coast of the United States to grazing land for cattle and settlements for people. Agriculture often takes over native habitats as farmers use land for grazing animals or planting **crops**. The timber industry cuts down acres of natural forests that are home to many species, too.

A preserved heath hen
credit: James St. John (CC BY 2.0)

Food chain disruption. An organism can face extinction through a more indirect route, too. The plucky little black-footed ferret, native to the American prairies, was declared extinct in the wild not once, but twice. The black-footed ferret depends on prairie dogs for food—a single ferret can eat up to 100 prairie dogs in one year. When people killed prairie dogs in massive numbers to use their habitat for grazing cattle, the black-footed ferret couldn't find enough food.

The black-footed ferret died off and was declared extinct in 1979.

PLANET EARTH

WORDS TO KNOW

conservation: managing and protecting natural resources.

preservation: to keep something protected for future generations.

sustainable: living in a way that has minimal long-term impact on the environment.

In 1981, a black-footed ferret showed up on someone's doorstep in Wyoming. Some ferrets were captured and brought into captivity to try to bring back the numbers. However, this population, too, had disappeared from the wild by 1987.

Natural extinction. Humans aren't the only reason species have faced extinction. Throughout Earth's history, climate changes and geological factors have also caused the extinction of species. The most talked-about extinction, of course, is the disappearance of the dinosaurs as a result of a meteor crashing to Earth. This meteor completely disrupted the cycles of the planet, causing mass extinctions.

GIVE THAT CROC A KISS

It's easy for people to get caught up in saving animals that we think are attractive, noble, or even cute and cuddly. But what about the ones that are downright unattractive or the ones that are deadly or fearsome to humans? These creatures need human help, too, if we're going to fight extinction. What's more, each of these animals is important to their ecosystem and to the earth as a balanced planet.

DID YOU KNOW? Christopher Columbus may have dined on the Puerto Rican hutia, a rodent many believe is now extinct.

See which species are currently endangered and critically endangered at this website. Do any of these surprise you?

WWF extinction

Steps to Extinction

The path to extinction can be relatively quick or it can take a very long time. But the end result is the same—extinction is forever. Here are the different stages of extinction.

> **Rare:** a relatively small number of individuals of the species exist.

> **Threatened:** the species probably will become endangered soon.

> **Endangered:** in danger of becoming extinct.

> **Extinct in the wild:** the only known individuals of the species are in captivity.

> **Extinct:** no known individuals of the species are left on the entire planet.

Plants don't escape the threat of extinction, either. Some species of cactus and lily are among the many plants that are threatened or endangered—again, mostly because of the loss of habitat as humans increasingly take over the land the plants need.

CONSERVATION AND PRESERVATION

Conservation and **preservation** involve protecting something, whether it's wildlife, plant life, a land area, or a natural resource. These practices can help the earth regain its natural balance. Conservation includes reducing the stress on land and wildlife and using **sustainable** management techniques. Preservation means keeping areas of land specifically for the use of the natural life within them.

Both conservation and preservation are critical to protecting the planet and everything that lives on it.

PLANET EARTH

> **WORDS TO KNOW**
>
> **wildlife refuge:** an area of protected land where species can live away from human intervention.
>
> **hydroponic:** growing plants in liquid, without using soil.

People are helping to save the endangered life on Earth in different ways. The best method involves protecting a species in its native habitat—by establishing an area as a **wildlife refuge**—or moving the species to a nature reserve.

Scientists are also trying to find new ways to increase food production for humans using less land. One way is through **hydroponics**, where plants grow without soil. The plants are given the nutrients they'd normally get from the soil through nutrient-rich water directly applied to their roots.

This way, plants can grow in places that are already developed, reducing the need for more and more land to be devoted to farming.

Hydroponics is growing plants without soil

credit: NASA/KSC

Finding the Balance

Mongolian wild horses were reintroduced to the wild
credit: A. Omer Karamollaoglu (CC BY 2.0)

The bald eagle regained its numbers
credit: dw_ross (CC BY 2.0)

SUCCESS STORIES

History has proven that when people decide to get involved and act, a species can be brought back from the brink of extinction—and even look forward to a very bright future. Przewalski's horse, also called the Mongolian wild horse or takhi, was extinct in the wild at one point.

Fortunately, several of the animals were in captivity. Otherwise, these stocky, spirited animals would be gone forever. In the 1990s, efforts were made to breed the remaining animals to build up their numbers, and eventually, they were reintroduced back into the wilds of Mongolia. Although these horses are still on the endangered list, scientists have high hopes for their future.

In 2007, the national symbol of America, the American bald eagle, was removed from the threatened list in the United States. In earlier decades, the chemical DDT had weakened the bald eagle's eggshells so much that birds weren't hatching.

PLANET EARTH

> **WORDS TO KNOW**
>
> **sanctuary:** a protected area that provides refuge for wildlife.

After the eagle was placed on the list and protected through the ban of DDT, the bird was able to start reproducing again successfully. Eventually, its numbers climbed.

The environment is an amazing, constantly changing place. It's incredible to think about all the elements that must come together to make a planet that can support life. And while we think of balance as something we need to try and achieve when it comes to the planet, it's a more complex process than simply labeling behavior as good or bad.

Some things that are usually good, such as water, can turn into a dangerous flood. And even events that seem harsh, such as a wildfire, can turn out to be good for nature. In some areas, such as the western United States, wildfires are important in nature's cycle because they eliminate overgrowth by burning it. Fire sparks new growth with what's left behind.

Your Turn

Try these methods of conserving and preserving—think globally and act locally!

› **Eat more local foods.** Visit a farmers' market or plant your own garden. If you have a lot of space, try getting your neighbors together to plant a community garden where everyone pitches in to plant, raise, harvest, and eat the produce. When you eat local foods, you're reducing the amount of fuel used to transport food from other areas.

› **Recycle, reuse, and cut down on unnecessary purchases.** By doing all of this, you reduce the amount of resources needed to make the stuff you use. This leaves more natural resources for the animals and plants.

› **Support national parks and wildlife preserves.** Visit or offer to volunteer however you can. Spread the word about these **sanctuaries** to get other people to understand and care about these treasured areas. Every state in America has at least one National Wildlife Refuge.

Finding the Balance

Elk stay safe in a river during a Montana forest fire
credit: John McColgan, U.S. Department of Agriculture

The year 2018 saw some of the largest and most destructive wildfires in California. As awful as they are to life and property, fire is an inevitable process in the natural life cycle of forests.

What's amazing is to realize just how much impact humans have on the environment—for better or for worse. With just one discovery or one invention, we can cause damage to our environment. But, as in nature, invention has a good side as well.

Humans can create things that help the environment or that heal the damage already done. And what's even more empowering is that we can all make choices and changes in our own lives that can have a lasting impact on our environment.

DID YOU KNOW?

President Teddy Roosevelt started the National Wildlife Refuge system in the United States in 1903.

PLANET EARTH

WORDS TO KNOW

geocaching: an outdoor treasure-hunting game using navigational techniques and clues to hide and seek containers called "geocaches" or "caches." A cache generally contains a logbook and "treasure," such as toys or trinkets.

Global Positioning System (GPS): a system of satellites, computers, and receivers that can determine the exact location of a receiver anywhere on the planet.

Learning about the challenges our environment faces shouldn't be all doom and gloom. As scientists and politicians learn more, countries are coming together to protect our planet by passing laws against dangerous practices and taking steps to manage our natural resources and protect what we have.

ESSENTIAL QUESTION

Think of one extinct species. How would life today be different if that species were still around?

Everyone plays a part in that process, so by learning all you can, you're already helping.

Geocache!

One of the most fun ways to get out and explore the natural world is by **geocaching**. With the help of a handheld **Global Positioning System (GPS)**, you seek out "caches," or treasure boxes, that other geocachers have hidden—all over the world! Usually, these caches are in natural settings, so if you start searching for them, you'll find yourself in parks and natural areas that you may not have even known were in your community. The best part—geocachers have made a pact with the environment. They don't hide boxes in areas that are disruptive to nature. They also have a "cache in, trash out" policy, which means they go hiking looking for treasure, but along the way, they clean up any litter that others have left behind. It's a great way to experience nature and help out at the same time.

 Find geocaches near you at this website.

geocaching

Activity

MAKE YOUR OWN HYDROPONIC PLANTER

One way humans may be able to protect our land in the future is to find new ways to grow food for the ever-growing human population. Using hydroponic planters on a large scale may offer a solution. Here's how you can make a very small version to see how they might work.

> **Caution:** Have an adult help you with this project, especially in making a hole in the bottle cap.

▶ **Cut a 2-liter bottle in half,** leaving the cap on. Make a hole or slit in the cap big enough for a cloth strip to fit through. Thread the strip through so that some cloth is in the upper part of the bottle and the rest comes out the top of the bottle through the cap.

▶ **Fill the bottom half of the bottle halfway with water.** Use litmus paper to test the pH of your water, following the instructions that came with the paper. Plants need a pH of between 5 and 7 to grow well. If your water isn't in this range, add a little squirt of lemon juice to increase the acidity (and lower the pH) or a sprinkle of baking soda to decrease the acidity (and raise the pH).

▶ **When your water is the right pH, add some plant nutrients.** Use the instructions on the nutrients container to figure out how much you need. Set this aside.

Project continues on next page . . .

109

Activity

> **Turn the top half of the bottle upside down.** Be sure your cotton material—the "wick"—is still in place, and fill the bottle half with your planting medium. The planting medium takes the place of soil, holding the plant upright. Ground coconut husks, called coco coir, is a popular choice. Tuck a plant runner or seeds in the middle of this material.

> **Set the top half of the bottle onto the bottom half.** Be sure the wick is far enough in both the top and bottom halves to transport water up to the plant. Check back in a little bit to see if the water is, indeed, moving up the wick to the plant. Change the water about once a week, making sure the new water is the right pH and has plant nutrients in it.

> **Once your plant's roots start getting bigger, take off the cap and remove the wick,** allowing the roots to reach down into the water. You'll need to oxygenate the water to prevent the roots from getting slimy. Cut a piece of aquarium tubing long enough to run down through the slit into the water. Either use a small air pump or a hollow rubber ball with the tubing poked into it for aeration. You'll need to "pump" the ball once a day to add oxygen to the water.

Think About It

Do you see how it would be possible to help the environment by using creative methods of growing food? Can you think of other ways, in addition to hydroponic planters, that we could save our natural resources but also meet the demands of feeding the human population?

GLOSSARY

abundant: a large amount.

accurate: true, correct.

acid rain: precipitation that has been polluted by acid.

acidic: describes a substance that is low on the pH scale and loses hydrogen in water. Examples of acidic substances include lemon juice and vinegar.

adapt: to make a change to better survive in the environment.

adaptation: the development of physical or behavioral changes to survive in an environment.

algae: a simple organism found in water that is like a plant but without roots, stems, or leaves.

alkaline: describes a substance that is high on the pH scale and gains hydrogen in water. Examples of basic substances include soap, baking soda, and ammonia.

amphibian: an animal with moist skin that is born in water but lives on land. An amphibian changes its body temperature by moving to warmer or cooler places. Frogs, toads, newts, efts, and salamanders are amphibians.

anaerobic: without oxygen. The opposite of aerobic, with oxygen.

ancestors: the people who lived before you.

aquatic: having to do with water.

atmosphere: the mixture of gases that surround a planet.

atom: the smallest particle of matter in the universe that makes up everything, like tiny building blocks or grains of sand.

axis: the imaginary line through the North and South Poles that the earth rotates around.

bacteria: tiny organisms found in soil, water, plants, and animals that are sometimes helpful and sometimes harmful.

beneficial: having good or helpful results.

biodegrade: to decay or break down naturally.

biome: a large natural area with a distinctive climate, geology, set of water resources, and group of plants and animals that are adapted for life there.

bird of prey: a bird that is a predator and eats other animals.

bounty: a gift or generous supply of something.

buoyant: light and floating.

by-product: an extra and sometimes unexpected or unintended result of an action or process.

camouflage: the colors or patterns that allow a plant or animal to blend in with its environment.

carbon dioxide: a gas formed by the burning of fossil fuels, the rotting of plants and animals, and the breathing out of animals, including humans.

carbon footprint: the total amount of carbon dioxide and other greenhouse gases emitted over the full life cycle of a product or service, or by a person or family in a year.

carnivore: an animal that eats only other animals.

cataract: a clouding of the eye's natural lens.

catastrophic: involving or causing large amounts of damage.

celestial body: a star, planet, moon, or other object in space.

cell: the basic building block of all living organisms.

chlorofluorocarbons (CFCs): simple gases that contain carbon, chlorine, fluorine, and sometimes hydrogen, that are a major cause of stratospheric ozone depletion.

chlorophyll: a pigment that makes plants green, used in photosynthesis to capture light energy.

class: a group of organisms with common attributes; a major category in grouping organisms.

classify: to put things in groups based on what they have in common.

clear-cut logging: a process in which all or almost all the trees in an area are chopped down.

climate: the average weather patterns in an area during a long period of time.

climate change: a change in long-term weather patterns, which happens through both natural and man-made processes.

GLOSSARY

combustion engine: an engine that burns fuel to produce energy.

compost: decayed food scraps and vegetation that can be put back in the soil or to recycle food scraps and vegetation and put them back in the soil.

condense: to change from a gas to a liquid.

coniferous: plants and trees that do not shed their leaves each year.

conservation: managing and protecting natural resources.

correlate: a relationship between two things that affect or impact one another.

crops: plants grown for food and other uses.

crude oil: petroleum oil as it comes out of the earth, before it is refined into other products.

current: the steady flow of water or air in one direction.

curvature: the amount something is curved.

debris: scattered pieces of waste or remains.

decay: to break down and rot.

deciduous: plants and trees that shed their leaves each year.

dense: tightly packed.

displace: to cause something to move from its usual or proper place.

diverse: a large variety.

dormant: in a state of rest or inactivity.

drought: a long period of little or no rain.

ecosystem: an interdependent community of living and nonliving things and their environment.

ectothermic: cold-blooded. Describes animals such as snakes that have a body temperature that varies with the surrounding temperature.

El Niño: unusually warm ocean conditions occurring every few years along the tropical west coast of South America. El Niño has dramatic affects on weather patterns around the world.

element: a substance that is made of one type of atom, such as iron, carbon, or oxygen.

emissions: something that is sent or given out, such as smoke, gas, heat, or light.

endangered: a species of plant or animal with a very low population that is at risk of disappearing entirely.

engineer: a person who uses science, math, and creativity to design and build things.

environment: everything in nature—living or nonliving—including plants, animals, rocks, and water.

equator: the imaginary line around the planet halfway between the North and South Poles.

evaporate: to convert from liquid to vapor.

exosphere: a very thin layer of gas surrounding a planet.

extinction: when a species dies out and there are no more left in the world.

extrude: when something is pushed or forced.

fertile: land that is good for growing plants.

flora: the plant life in an ecosystem.

food chain: a community of animals and plants where each is eaten by another higher up in the chain.

food web: a network of connected food chains.

fossil: the remains of any organism, including animals and plants, that have been preserved in rock.

fungi: mold, mildew, rust, and mushrooms. Plural of fungus.

geocaching: an outdoor treasure-hunting game using navigational techniques and clues to hide and seek containers called "geocaches" or "caches." A cache generally contains a logbook and "treasure," such as toys or trinkets.

geology: the rocks, minerals, and physical structure of an area.

gills: filter-like structures that let an organism get oxygen out of the water to breathe.

glacier: an enormous mass of frozen snow and ice that moves across the earth's surface.

Global Positioning System (GPS): a system of satellites, computers, and receivers that can determine the exact location of a receiver anywhere on the planet.

global warming: an increase in the average temperature of the earth's atmosphere, enough to cause climate change.

GLOSSARY

glucose: a type of sugar a plant makes for food.

greenhouse effect: when the presence in the atmosphere of gases such as carbon dioxide, water vapor, and methane allow incoming sunlight to pass through, but absorb heat radiated back from the earth's surface, trapping solar radiation.

greenhouse gas: a gas that traps heat in the earth's atmosphere and contributes to the greenhouse effect and global warming.

habitat: a plant or animal's home, which supplies it with food, water, and shelter.

hazardous waste: a waste with properties that make it dangerous or capable of having a harmful effect on human health or the environment.

herbicide: a chemical used to kill unwanted plants such as weeds.

herbivore: an animal that eats only plants.

homeotherm: an organism that can regulate its own body temperature.

horizon: the line in the distance where the land or sea seems to meet the sky.

hydroelectricity: electricity created by the flow of water.

hydroponic: growing plants in liquid, without using soil.

hydrothermal vent: a crack in the sea floor where super-heated fluid comes out.

industry: the large-scale production of goods, especially in factories.

invasive species: a plant or animal species that enters an ecosystem and spreads quickly, harming the system's balance.

kelp: large brown seaweed that grows in shallow ocean depths. It forms extensive forests that provide habitat for a wide variety of organisms.

kingdom: a broad division of living organisms.

landfill: a huge area of land where trash gets buried.

leaf litter: fallen leaves and other dead plant material that is starting to break down.

lichen: a plant-like organism made of algae and fungus that grows on solid surfaces such as rocks or trees.

magnify: to enlarge.

maize: corn.

mammal: a type of animal, such as a human, dog, or cat. Mammals are born live, feed milk to their young, and usually have hair or fur covering most of their skin.

marine: of or relating to the ocean.

mesosphere: the atmosphere above the stratosphere but below the thermosphere.

meteor: a streak of light produced when a small particle from outer space enters the earth's atmosphere.

microbe: a tiny living or nonliving thing. Another word for microorganism.

mid-latitudes: the areas halfway between the equator and the North and South Poles.

migration: moving from one place to another, often with the change in seasons.

Milky Way: the galaxy that contains our solar system.

minerals: nutrients found in rocks and soil that keep plants and animals healthy and growing. Salt and nitrogen are two minerals.

molecule: a group of atoms bound together. Molecules combine to form matter.

natural resource: a material such as coal, timber, water, or land that is found in nature and is useful to humans.

nocturnal: describes an animal that is active at night instead of during the day.

nutrients: substances that living things need to live and grow.

organic: something that is or was living, such as wood, paper, grass, insects, and animals.

organism: a living thing, such as a plant or animal.

overhunting: when an animal is hunted in great numbers, so much that their population falls to low levels. This can cause extinction.

oxygen: the most abundant element on Earth, found in the air and in the water.

ozone: a gas that is a major air pollutant in the lower atmosphere but a beneficial part of the middle atmosphere. The ozone layer blocks most of the sun's ultraviolet radiation.

GLOSSARY

ozone depletion: the thinning of the ozone layer.

permeable: a substance that liquid (or gas) can flow through.

pesticide: a chemical used to kill pests such as rodents or insects.

pH: a measure of acidity or alkalinity, on a scale from 0 (most acidic) to 14 (most alkaline).

photosynthesis: the process plants use to turn sunlight, carbon dioxide, and water into food.

phylum chordata: a large group in the animal kingdom. It includes mammals, birds, fish, reptiles, and amphibians. These animals all have spinal cords.

plankton: microscopic plants and animals that float or drift in great numbers in bodies of water.

pollutant: a substance that pollutes, or dirties, the planet.

precipitation: the falling to Earth of rain, snow, or any form of water.

precycling: buying less and creating less waste.

predator: an animal or plant that kills and eats another animal.

preen: when birds groom their feathers with their beaks.

preservation: to keep something protected for future generations.

propagate: to grow, to increase the amount of something.

radiation: the process of energy from light or sound moving from its source, such as the sun, radiating outward.

recycling: shredding, squashing, pulping, or melting items to use the materials to create new products.

renewable: something that isn't used up, that can be replaced.

reptile: an animal covered with scales that crawls on its belly or on short legs. A reptile changes its body temperature by moving to warmer or cooler places. Snakes, turtles, lizards, alligators, and crocodiles are reptiles.

respiratory: having to do with breathing.

rotation: a turn all the way around.

runoff: produced when water picks up wastes as it flows over the surface of the ground. Runoff can pollute streams, lakes, rivers, and oceans.

rural: areas in the countryside.

sanctuary: a protected area that provides refuge for wildlife.

Santa Ana winds: Southern California winds that occur when air changes temperature while moving over mountains.

savanna: a dry, rolling grassland with scattered shrubs and trees.

sediment: material deposited by water, wind, or glaciers.

sewage: waste from buildings, carried away through sewers.

smog: fog combined with smoke or other pollutants.

solar power: energy from the sun converted to electricity.

solar system: the eight planets and their moons that orbit the sun.

species: a group of closely related and physically similar organisms.

stomata: tiny pores on the outside of leaves that allow gases and water vapor to pass in and out.

stratosphere: the middle region of the atmosphere, where the ozone layer is.

suburban: having to do with living areas at the edges of cities.

sundial: a tool that uses a shadow cast by the sun to determine the time.

sustainable: living in a way that has minimal long-term impact on the environment.

symbiosis: a relationship between two different species of organisms in which each benefits from the other.

temperate: describes a climate or weather that is not extreme.

thermosphere: the thickest part of the atmosphere, rising more than 300 miles above the surface of Earth.

trade winds: winds that blow almost continually toward the equator from the northeast north of the equator and from the southeast south of the equator.

GLOSSARY

tropics: the area near the equator.

troposphere: the lowest part of the earth's atmosphere, where most weather occurs.

tundra: a treeless Arctic region that is permanently frozen below the top layer of soil.

turbine: a machine with rotating blades that changes one type of energy to another, such as wind energy into electricity.

ultraviolet (UV): invisible light radiated from the sun.

urban: relating to a city or large town.

vapor: a substance suspended in the air as a gas, such as steam, mist, or fog.

vegetation: all plant life in an area.

vermicomposting: using worms in compost to break down and recycle food wastes.

vertebrate: an organism with a backbone or spinal column.

virus: a non-living microbe that can cause disease.

vitamin D: a vitamin that is important for bones and teeth. It is found in egg yolks and milk, and it can be produced in the body from sunlight.

water cycle: the process where the planet's water evaporates, condenses, and returns to Earth.

water table: the underground water supply for the planet.

wavelength: the spacing of sound or light waves.

wetland: an area where the land is soaked with water. Wetlands are often important habitats for fish, plants, and wildlife.

wildlife refuge: an area of protected land where species can live away from human intervention.

yellow dwarf: a small star, such as our own sun.

Metric Conversions

Use this chart to find the metric equivalents to the English measurements in this book. If you need to know a half measurement, divide by two. If you need to know twice the measurement, multiply by two. How do you find a quarter measurement? How do you find three times the measurement?

English	Metric
1 inch	2.5 centimeters
1 foot	30.5 centimeters
1 yard	0.9 meter
1 mile	1.6 kilometers
1 pound	0.5 kilogram
1 teaspoon	5 milliliters
1 tablespoon	15 milliliters
1 cup	237 milliliters

RESOURCES

BOOKS

Animal Antipodes: Global Opposites, Carly Allen-Fletcher, Creston Books (September 2018), 1939547490

Biodiversity: Explore the Diversity of Life on Earth with Environmental Science Activities for Kids (Build It Yourself), Laura Perdew, Nomad Press (March 2019), 1619307510

Earth: By the Numbers, Steve Jenkins, HMH Books for Young Readers (July 2019), B07FK78BW9

Eyes on Insects, Ruth Strother, Silver Dolphin Books (May 2019), 1684123151

Funky Junk: Recycle Rubbish into Art!, Gary Kings, Dover Publications (August 2012), 048649022X

Human Footprint: Everything You Will Eat, Use, Wear, Buy, and Throw Out in Your Lifetime, Ellen Kirk, National Geographic Kids (March 2011), 9781426307676

Recycle This Book: 100 Top Children's Book Authors Tell You How to Go Green, Yearling (March 2009), B002361NG4

Solar Energy: Putting the Sun to Work, Jessie Alkire, Super Sandcastle (September 2018), 1532115741

Water Energy: Putting Water to Work, Jessie Alkire, Super Sandcastle (September 2018), 153211575X

World Wildlife Fund for Nature, Kirsty Holmes, Booklife (June 2019), 1786373157

RESOURCES

WEBSITES

Britannica Kids:
kids.britannica.com/kids/article/environment/399445

Conservation Kids (U.S. Fish & Wildlife Services):
fws.gov/international/education-zone/conservation-kids.html

EPA for Kids: *epa.gov/students*

National Audubon Society Kids:
web4.audubon.org/educate/kids

National Institute of Environmental Health Science:
kids.niehs.nih.gov/index.htm

National Wildlife Federation for Kids:
nwf.org/kids-and-family

National Resources Defense Council: *nrdc.org*

Ranger Rick: *rangerrick.org*

RESOURCES

QR CODE GLOSSARY

page 3: climatecentral.org/news/history-global-warming-animation-21670

page 7: jsc.nasa.gov/history/mission_trans/apollo8.htm

page 9: youtube.com/watch?v=GcbU4bfkDA4

page 20: scihi.org/joseph-priestley-discovery-oxygen

page 25: earth.nullschool.net

page 26: oceanweather.com/data

page 28: getty.edu/art/collection/objects/1196/attributed-to-bernard-palissy-oval-basin-french-about-1550/?dz=0.3605,0.3666,1.39

page 33: khanacademy.org/partner-content/nova/energy/v/windpower

page 39: pbs.org/video/nova-solar-power

page 51: smithsonianmag.com/videos/category/science/slo-mo-footage-of-a-bumble-bee-dislodging-pollen

page 63: youtube.com/watch?v=fWkeJREta_I

page 66: watersgeo.epa.gov/mywaterway/mywaterway.html

page 67: epa.gov/cleanups/cleanups-my-community

page 73: climate.nasa.gov/vital-signs/global-temperature

page 77: carbonfootprint.com/calculator.aspx

page 80: ozonewatch.gsfc.nasa.gov/ozone_maps/movies/OZONE_D1979-07%25P1Y_G%5e1280X720.IOMPS_PNPP_V21_MMERRA2_LSH.mp4

page 88: youtube.com/watch?v=cHWYoDKYnQo

page 89: youtube.com/watch?v=2c8YxMb0tlk

page 95: youtube.com/watch?v=Gwk1B66dvAM

page 102: worldwildlife.org/species/directory?direction=desc&sort=extinction_status

page 108: geocaching.com/play

RESOURCES

ESSENTIAL QUESTIONS

Introduction: What type of environment do you live in? Desert, tundra, forest, grassland?

Chapter 1: What are some of the ways the environment where you live maintains its balance? What happens if that balance wobbles?

Chapter 2: How are air and water part of the same system?

Chapter 3: How do you think life on Earth would be different if we were closer to the sun? What if we were farther away?

Chapter 4: What would happen if a species were suddenly gone from the earth?

Chapter 5: Do you think it's possible for humans to live on Earth and not produce a single bit of pollution?

Chapter 6: Why is it difficult for some people to believe that climate change is a concern?

Chapter 7: Do you think everyone on the planet could stop buying new products for an entire week? What impact would that have on our environment?

Chapter 8: Think of one extinct species. How would life today be different if that species were still around?

INDEX

A

acid rain, 60, 67
activities
    Air Pollution Collection Cards, 70
    Do Some Vermicomposting, 96–97
    Global Warming in a Jar, 84
    Is It Acidic?, 34
    Make Your Own Backyard Pond, 14–15
    Make Your Own Biodiversity Journal, 55
    Make Your Own Effects of Acids Experiment, 69
    Make Your Own Giant Air Blaster, 33
    Make Your Own Heat Transfer Project, 46
    Make Your Own Hydroponic Planter, 109–110
    Make Your Own Miniature Water Cycle, 35
    Make Your Own Naturally Dyed Shopping Tote, 95
    Make Your Own Ozone Depletion Experiment, 86
    Make Your Own Scratch-and-Sniff Recycled Paper, 98
    Make Your Own Solar Chimney, 45
    Make Your Own Solar-Powered Oven, 44
    Make Your Own Tullgren Funnel, 16–17
    Pond Exploration Kit, 54
    Propagate Your Own Tree, 85
    Watch Plants Breathe, 32
    Whole World Granola, 18
air
    atmosphere, 19–24. *See also* ozone
    greenhouse gases/effect, iv, v, 71, 73–76. *See also* carbon dioxide
    oxygen, 20–23, 32, 38, 75, 79
    pollution, 60–63, 70, 74–76, 79–80
    wind, 24–28, 33, 38
animals. *See also* insects
    adaptations of, 53
    air/atmosphere for, 19, 21
    classification of, 48–50
    climate change affecting, 72, 82
    environment for, 1–2. *See also* biomes; habitats
    extinction of, 99–103
    in food chains/webs, 8–9, 11, 17, 38, 52, 64, 66–67, 83, 101–102
    pollution affecting, 58, 64, 66–68, 70
    recycling by, 93–94, 96–97
    sun's importance to, 8, 38
    symbiosis with, 51
    water for, 28–29
aquatic biomes, 13, 14–15. *See also* oceans

B

balance, 8–9, 99–108
biomes, 7, 10–17, 47

C

carbon dioxide, iv–v, 21–22, 28, 38, 61, 62, 74–77, 79
carbon footprint, 77
chlorofluorocarbons (CFCs), 76, 79–80, 81
climate change, v, 3–5, 31, 62, 71–86
composting/vermicomposting, 90–94, 96–97
conservation efforts, iv, 76–79, 87–98, 103–110

D

deserts, 10–11, 13, 28, 47
direction, sun for, 42
droughts, 72–73

INDEX

E

Earth
   air and water. *See* air; water
   balance on, 8–9, 99–108
   environmental issues, 2–5. *See also* climate change; conservation efforts; pollution
   environment on, 1–2. *See also* biomes; habitats
   life on. *See* animals; insects; life on Earth; plants
   in solar system, iv, 4, 6–8. *See also* sun
energy sources, iv–v, 27–28, 33, 38–40, 44–46, 61–63, 67–68, 74, 83, 88. *See also* food chains/webs; sun
environment, 1–2. *See also* biomes; habitats
environmental issues, 2–5. *See also* climate change; conservation efforts; pollution
extinction, 99–103

F

farming/agriculture, 12, 36, 65, 72, 83, 101, 104, 108–110
floods, 4, 73, 106
food chains/webs, 8–9, 11, 17, 38, 52, 64, 66–67, 83, 101–102
forests, 7, 10–11, 13, 47
fossil fuels, iv, 28, 39–40, 61–63, 67–68, 74, 83, 88

G

geocaching, 108
glaciers, 31, 47
glass, v, 89
grasslands, 10–11, 13
greenhouse gases/effect, iv, v, 71, 73–76. *See also* carbon dioxide

H

habitats, 9, 13, 14, 29, 50, 70, 78, 101, 103–104

I

insects, 7, 16, 51–52, 65, 76, 93
invasive species, 53, 55, 100

L

land pollution, v, 57–59, 60
life on Earth.
   See also animals; insects; plants
   adaptations of, 53
   air and water for. *See* air; water
   classification of, 48–50
   climate change affecting, 72, 75, 79, 82–83
   conservation efforts, iv, 76–79, 87–98, 103–110
   environment for, 1–2.
     See also biomes; habitats
   extinction of, 99–103
   food chains/webs for, 8–9, 11, 17, 52, 64, 66–67, 83, 101–102
   pollution affecting, 58, 64, 66–68, 70, 75
   recycling by, 93–94, 96–97
   solar system and, 6–8
   sun's importance to, 7, 8, 22, 30, 36, 38
   symbiosis with, 51

M

metal, v, 90
methane, 74, 75, 76
mountains, 2, 10–11

N

nitrous oxide, 74, 76
noise pollution, 70

O

oceans, 10, 13, 25–26, 29–30, 39, 47, 66, 67–68
oil spills, v, 67–68
oxygen, 20–23, 32, 38, 75, 79
ozone, 23–24, 43, 63, 76, 79–82, 86

INDEX

P

paper, v, 88, 89, 91, 98
Paris Agreement, v, 62
plants. *See also* farming/agriculture
  adaptations of, 53
  air/atmosphere for, 19, 21–22, 32, 75, 79
  classification of, 48–49
  climate change affecting, 72, 75, 79, 82–83
  environment for, 1–2. *See also* biomes; habitats
  extinction of, 100, 103
  in food chains/webs, 8–9, 11, 17, 38, 52, 64, 67, 83
  pollution affecting, 64, 67, 75
  sun's importance to, 8, 22, 36, 38
  symbiosis with, 51
  water for, 28–29
plastic, v, 58–59, 88, 89, 91–92
pollution, 24, 56–70
  air, 60–63, 70, 74–76, 79–80
  land, v, 57–59, 60
  noise, 70
  water, v, 64–68
precycling, 94

R

rainforests, 7, 47
recycling, 87–98
renewable energy, iv–v, 27–28, 33, 38–40, 44–46

S

solar system, iv, 4, 6–8. *See also* sun
sun, iv–v, 7, 8, 20, 22, 30, 35, 36–46, 63, 71, 79–84
symbiosis, 51

T

time, telling, 40–42
timeline, iv–v
tundra, 10, 12, 13, 28, 47

U

ultraviolet (UV) rays, 20, 23, 43, 63, 79–83

W

water
  acidity of, 34, 60, 67
  aquatic biomes, 13, 14–15. *See also* oceans
  cycle, 7, 20, 28–30, 35, 39, 66, 92
  droughts with lack of, 72–73
  floods, 4, 73, 106
  oxygen in, 21
  pollution, v, 64–68
weather, 4, 10, 19, 20, 25–26, 29–30, 73. *See also* acid rain; climate change
wildfires, 4, 60, 106, 107
wind, 24–28, 33, 38